KAYLA O'BRIAN
AND THE DANGEROUS JOURNEY

Other Crossway Books by
Hilda Stahl

THE PRAIRIE FAMILY ADVENTURE SERIES

Sadie Rose and the Daring Escape
Sadie Rose and the Cottonwood Creek Orphan
Sadie Rose and the Outlaw Rustlers
Sadie Rose and the Double Secret
Sadie Rose and the Mad Fortune Hunters

THE SUPER J*A*M SERIES

The Great Adventures of Super J*A*M
The World's Greatest Hero

GROWING UP ADVENTURES

Sendi Lee Mason and the Milk Carton Kids
Sendi Lee Mason and the Stray Striped Cat

Kayla O'Brian
AND THE
DANGEROUS JOURNEY

Hilda Stahl

CROSSWAY BOOKS • WHEATON, ILLINOIS
A DIVISION OF GOOD NEWS PUBLISHERS

Cover design: Ad Plus

Cover illustration: David Acquistapace

First printing, 1990

Second printing, 1994

Printed in the United States of America

Library of Congress Catalog Card Number 90-80618

ISBN 0-89107-577-1

J
F
STAHL
11.18.2011

*Dedicated with love
to my three beautiful and brilliant
daughters*

Laurie Ann
Sonya Lorraine
Evangelynn Kaye

Between the years 1854 and 1904 the Children's Aid Society found homes in Midwest states for over 100,000 homeless New York City street children. Some of them went willingly, others didn't. Some of them were taken in by wonderful families, others weren't. The Children's Aid Society wanted a better life for the orphans — and some of them found it.

Kayla pressed her hand over her nose to keep from retching at the terrible smells as she ran through the alley beside Timothy to take Sean Murphy's dinner to him. She hated the alley, but it was a shortcut to the docks, and Hope Murphy wouldn't hear of her husband going hungry—him being the hard worker that he was.

At the sound of pounding hooves Kayla looked over her shoulder, then gasped in alarm. A man astride a great roan leaned low in the saddle and was galloping at breakneck speed toward them. She jerked Timothy out of the way just as the roan galloped past. Kayla felt the heat of the horse's flank and the rush of wind. Her knees almost buckled, but she stiffened her legs and her spine as well. It wouldn't do to let Timothy know how frightened she felt, how frightened she'd felt the past weeks.

"Watch where you're going!" shouted Timothy, his blue eyes blazing with anger. He never was one to keep his temper.

Kayla flushed with embarrassment. They'd been taught better manners than that, but in the two weeks since the boat had landed in New York City her brother had picked up some of the ways of the other lads that ran the streets. She tugged at his dirty sleeve. "Don't be shoutin' now, Timothy. It's not a thing to do, you know."

He grinned impishly. She was fourteen years old, just a year to the day older than he, but she felt it was her place to point out his misdeeds. "Don't I know now. You've told me often enough, don't you think?"

Before she could respond, the great roan reared with a shrill scream. Kayla watched two ragamuffins, six or maybe seven years old, pitching stones at the roan. One boy's left ear was half-gone. The other boy had a withered hand. The rider's long coattails billowed out as he lost his seat, then slammed back into the saddle. The man's fancy bowler flew off his head and landed on a pile of rubbish. The roan's hooves crashed to the bricks, then again it reared up, this time spilling its rider onto the refuse scattered across the bricks. The roan's front hooves came down again and missed the boys by the width of a hair. Kayla's heart leaped to her throat. The boys cried out and ducked around the side of the building into the crowded, noisy street and away from the crazed horse. The rider lay motionless against the brick building. The roan kicked a box, splintering the wood. Trembling, Kayla hung back with Timothy close at her side as the horse bucked and snorted. The boys peeked around the corner of the building, then dashed to the fallen rider to go through his pockets.

"Get away from him, you thieves!" shouted Kayla as she ducked away from the roan's hooves. Her voice was lost in the neigh of the horse and the pounding of its hooves. She looked around for a weapon even though she was bigger than the boys. She'd already learned that many of the street boys carried knives for protection. She knew they wouldn't hesitate to use it on her if she got in their way.

As the roan bucked past, Timothy grabbed for the dangling reins. "Settle down, big fellow. I won't let them hurt you again."

The roan's eyes rolled and it bobbed its great head, almost lifting Timothy off his feet.

While Timothy calmed the roan, Kayla grabbed a splintered board and ran toward the fallen rider, shouting at the boys. They turned and saw her, then scrambled angrily away, yelling words back at her that burned her ears. She knelt in the dirt beside the rider. He moaned, and she held her hand against his wide shoulder to keep him from moving. Blood oozed from a cut on the side of his head. "You've got quite a lump there, sir," she said. "Just lie still a bit and I'll see if you've broken anything."

He turned his head so he could see her.

She surmised he was a man past his prime, but still lean and muscled. His once-clean clothes showed that he was a man of means. He scowled, his eyes dark with pain. "Don't touch me, you guttersnipe!"

Kayla jerked to her full height and lifted her chin. The string that held back her long black hair slipped out, and her hair cascaded around her thin shoulders and over her ragged dress. Pride flashed in her clear blue eyes. "Sir, I am no guttersnipe!" But she knew she looked like one. She had been saving her good dress to wear when they reached Briarwood, a horse farm in Maryland. On the trip from Ireland she'd outgrown all of her dresses, and the one she wore now was Mama's. Abruptly Kayla's mind leaped away from thoughts of Mama. She turned her full attention back to the hurt rider, who was struggling to his feet no matter what she had said.

He patted his breast pocket, then frowned at Kayla. "You didn't rob me."

"No, but two scalawags were about to, and I put a stop to it," she said, brushing her long hair out of her eyes.

Timothy walked the roan to the man. "Here's your gelding, sir. You should be proud of this fine piece of horseflesh."

The man grabbed the reins. "I don't understand why you didn't take my money and my horse."

As Kayla handed the man his hat and he clamped it on his gray head, she looked him right in the eyes. "Our Lord Jesus wouldn't want us to be stealing anything, sir."

Timothy squared his shoulders. He was small for his age, yearning for the day he'd be a big strapping man like Papa had been. "We are O'Brians of County Offaly, and we don't steal, sir."

"So you say," said the man gruffly. He swung into the saddle. "Let me give you two O'Brians a piece of advice: Get off the streets. Live on the streets long enough and you won't remember that you don't steal. You'll steal to survive. You'll lie and cheat and maybe even kill. Anything to survive."

Kayla knotted her fists at her sides. "Let me give you a piece of advice, sir. Don't gallop your roan at full speed through the streets of New York City or you just might kill someone."

He flushed. "I was late for an appointment."

"And now are later still," said Kayla.

The man nodded. "Take my advice and get off the streets. Contact the Children's Aid Society for help." He kneed the roan and rode out of the alley into the noisy street.

Kayla shivered. "We must get to Maryland, Timothy."

"I know," he whispered.

"But first we must deliver dinner to Sean Murphy." Kayla laughed, and her blue eyes twinkled.

In his rush to get away from his six crying, hungry kids, Sean Murphy had walked away without the thick slices of bread smeared with lard and the two apples his wife had packed him. On making their own dinner Mrs. Murphy had noticed the sugar sack of food, so sent Kayla to run it to the docks. Timothy had gone with her since it was not right for a girl to be on her own in such a city.

At the docks they found Sean Murphy, a tall, broad man with a thick beard. His clothes were wet with sweat even though it was a cool September day. "You saved me life, you two did," he said in his hearty voice. "My belly was touching to my backbone for sure."

Timothy's stomach growled as he watched Sean Murphy wolf down the bread and lard. Since they'd left County Offaly he couldn't remember a time that he hadn't been hungry. Maybe on Briarwood Farms he'd get enough food to fill him.

Kayla watched the sea gulls dip and fly, filling the air with their cries. She was hungry, but she didn't want bread and lard again. She wanted fresh vegetables from the garden they'd left behind. On Briarwood Farms she was sure they'd have vegetables. She turned back to Sean. "Sean Murphy . . ." she said as he swallowed his last bite.

"What, girl?"

"When can we be on our way to Maryland?"

"Soon, girl, soon."

"But you said that yesterday, Sean Murphy," said Kayla.

"I know, girl." He wiped his mouth with the back of his large work-roughened hand. "I talked to a man just today who said you could catch a ride on his boat all the way to Baltimore. I got to find a way for you to get from there to Briarwood Farms."

"We could walk," said Timothy. "We're great ones for hiking."

Kayla nodded. She didn't care how they got there, just so they did.

"Your papa wouldn't want me sending you off without making plans for you to get there safe and sound, now would he?" Sean Murphy slipped one muscled arm around Kayla and the other around Timothy and pulled them close as he talked about how he felt obligated to help them.

Kayla smelled his sweat and dirt and felt his love for them. He really did care. Papa had made friends with him on the way over. Papa had worked with horses all his life, and Sean Murphy had worked the docks. But they both loved Ireland and hated leaving, but had done so because it was best for their families.

Tears burned Kayla's eyes, and she turned to look up at the gray sky. She must not think about Papa. That would come later — in Maryland. Wind blew cool air off the water. Men scurried around, loading boats, yelling and laughing.

"You two best be getting back or Hope will be worrying over you," said Sean Murphy. He hugged them close, then let them go.

Kayla walked around a stack of barrels as she struggled against the bad thoughts she was having about Hope Murphy. Sean Murphy was a man full of love, but his tired wife was another matter altogether. Six children with another on the way, plus the move from Ireland, had drained everything out of her. She had thought they'd live in a big house with a big yard, but they lived in one small room in a tenement building that wasn't fit for rats, let alone people. Kayla knew Hope had let Sean Murphy take them in only because she wanted to please him.

Timothy kicked at a piece of broken brick. "I wonder if the Children's Aid Society could help us get to Maryland."

Kayla frowned. "And why are you saying that, Timothy?"

"I have a feeling deep in here." He thumped his chest over his heart.

Kayla stopped. "What feeling, Timothy?"

He sighed heavily. "Kayla girl, I have a feeling that we'll never see Briarwood Farms."

"Don't say that!" She gripped his arm as shivers ran up and down her spine. Sometimes Timothy seemed to know things ahead of time, just like Mama had.

"Don't let me frighten you, Kayla." Timothy laughed, but Kayla knew it was forced. "We'll get to Briarwood Farms. That's just what we'll do all right."

Later, in the middle of the night, Kayla thought of Timothy's words again, and she shivered. Sean Murphy's snores almost blew the door open, with quieter snores coming from Timothy and two of the Murphy children keeping time with Sean's.

Kayla crept from her mat near the door out to the worn step. She huddled into her blanket against the chilly breeze. She wanted to breathe deeply, the way she had at home in Ireland, but she figured nobody could breathe deep here, not with all the odors of New York City. Here soot and smoke filled the air. It was a noisy place too. Horses whinnied, and their hooves clopped along the brick streets. Wagons and drays bumped along behind the horses. Street boys shouted to each other. Fiddle music sounded low and mournful, then light and airy. Night sounds were almost as loud as the noise of broad daylight.

"I must be getting me and Timothy to Maryland where we belong," she whispered. "A body could shrivel up and die here."

Sudden tears pricked her eyes, and she quickly brushed them away. It wouldn't do to feel sorry for herself, or for her brother for that matter. They had their health and their youth, and even better, they had God on their side. What more could they want or need? But she knew what more she desperately wanted and needed. She tried to push those thoughts aside, but couldn't.

"Maryland we need. And fresh air," she said with an impish grin. "Tomorrow we'll gather our stuff and tell Sean Murphy we'll be leaving no matter what."

Kayla woke with a start to find a crying baby crawling over her legs and a jabbering toddler tugging on her mass of raven-black hair. Shouts from other tenants drifted through the thin walls. Smells of baking bread, frying potatoes and onions, and coffee mixed with the odors of a wet bed, dirty bodies, and cooking porridge in the Murphys' room. The toddler tangled a strand of Kayla's hair around her chubby fingers and tugged. Kayla winced in pain, then carefully worked her hair free. She glanced across to where Timothy's mat was. He was already gone. Her heart sank.

Silently she prayed, "Heavenly Father, keep my Timothy pure in heart and safe from all harm." He was thirteen and needed a firm hand that only Papa could give him. Tears welled up in Kayla's eyes, and she blinked fast to blink them away.

"Mary girl," Kayla said as she reached for the crying baby, "come tell me what it is that's making you cry this early in the morn." She swung the baby high. "Oh, 'tis a wet one we have here." Kayla patted the toddler's head. "Go fetch me a dry nappy, will you now, Angel?"

"Nappy," said Angel. She balanced herself with her arms spread as she walked across three empty mats and four with sleeping children to the pile of folded rags that they used for the baby.

Just then the door opened, letting in a rush of cold air. Hope Murphy stepped inside, her face flushed and her breathing ragged. She sank to a chair and breathed deeply.

"You look as if you've been running," said Kayla in a happy voice. She had promised herself that she'd be cheerful and kind no matter what.

"That I have," said Hope Murphy, wiping her forehead with the tail of her faded apron. "A dog grabbed a loaf of bread right out of my hands, and I chased it all the way to the livery."

"Did you catch it?"

"No. And it was bread for our breakfast!"

"We still have the porridge," said Kayla.

"That we do." Hope pushed herself up awkwardly and smoothed her apron over her rounded stomach. "I shouldn't have chased that mutt, what with the new babe coming any day now." She sighed heavily. "And just look at us . . . crowded in here without a spare bit of space."

Kayla blushed with guilt as she glanced over at the boxes of stuff that belonged to them. She knew without herself, Timothy, and their things the Murphy family would have more room. "Hope Murphy, we do plan to be out of here soon. Today, I'm hoping."

"I don't feel right in pushing you poor little orphans out, but it's too hard to have you here."

Kayla's head spun at being called a "poor little orphan." Hope's voice faded in and out as she talked and dished up porridge. Automatically Kayla fed the baby some porridge, but couldn't swallow a bite of her own. She quickly divided it between the three little boys and Sara, who wolfed hers down and wanted more. But there was no more, and they turned away hungry as usual. They wrestled across the mats, while Kayla tried to roll them up and stack them against the wall.

As quickly as she could, she took her Bible and sat on the step to read to gain the strength she'd need for the day. Feeding her spirit was important, but oh how she wanted to feed her body too!

She read in Matthew about the miracles that Jesus performed, then gazed down the cluttered, noisy street. "We need a miracle, we do, Jesus," she whispered. "Me and Timothy do. We must get to Maryland."

The three little boys burst out the door, knocking against Kayla. Shouting, they ran down to the third doorway, pounded on the door, and called for Gunther to come out to play.

Anger at the boys rose in her, and she bowed her head. "Forgive my anger, Lord Jesus. Keep my heart pure before You. And thank You, dear Jesus, that You will show us the way to Maryland. I need to hear the beautiful silence of the country and walk through the rich grass and smell fresh air like we had in Ireland. And a bite to eat would be good too."

She retied the string on her hair that badly needed washing and combing. Her stomach growled with hunger as she retied her faded apron that once had been Mama's.

"Kayla!" shouted Timothy as he ran down the street, his hands behind his back. "I brought you something. Wait'll you see."

She stood and waited, smiling at the flash of excitement in Timothy's blue eyes. His raven-black hair needed trimming, and she promised herself she'd get the shears to it soon. "What is it you have for me, Timothy?"

He stopped in front of her, his chest out with pride and

a wide smile on his narrow face. "This!" He held a gunnysack out to her. "Don't be frightened to look inside. It's not a viper, you know."

She held the sack and opened it slowly, then gasped at the sight of fresh fruit and vegetables. "Oh, Timothy! Where did you get it?"

"I bought it at the market."

"But you had no money!"

"I ran to the market early and helped the merchants. They paid me in goods." He swaggered forward. His shirt and pants were dirty and ripped, and his shoes had holes in the toes, but he felt like a man of great wealth. He'd brought a bunch of carrots, a head of cabbage, an onion, several apples, turnips, ears of corn with light brown silks and green husks, and two pears. "I knew you yearned for more than bread and lard to eat."

"That I did." Kayla lifted out an apple, rubbed it against her apron, and bit into it with a snap. Juice hit her face and her hand, and she giggled. She sat on the step with Timothy beside her, and they ate an apple and a pear each. "Thank You, Jesus, for one miracle," she said as she looked up at the smoky sky. "Thank You for fresh food."

Timothy frowned slightly. "I brought the food, Kayla."

"That I know, Timothy, but Jesus gave you the idea to go to the market and the strength to do the work."

Timothy grinned and nodded. "That He did."

"And He'll give us yet another miracle," said Kayla. "He'll get us to wide open places with a sky as blue as your eyes and horses for us to tend and cows that give milk for us to drink . . . And real butter, and even cream for our porridge."

Timothy twisted the toe of his shoe against the brick at his feet. "This morn Sean Murphy wanted Papa's letter from

Briarwood Farms to show the man at the dock. I looked in the stuff Papa tucked away, but I could not find the letter that tells about Briarwood Farms. I couldn't find it at all."

Kayla patted her mouth with the tail of her apron and pushed back the strange feeling that rose inside her. "It has to be there, Timothy. Could be you overlooked it in your haste."

"It wasn't there, Kayla O'Brian. I know that for certain."

"What are you thinking, Timothy O'Brian?"

"Hope Murphy has always thought it was beyond her husband to bother with us going to Maryland. Maybe she destroyed it."

"That I will not believe!"

"It's not in you to think ill of anyone, Kayla."

"But it is in you? Is that what you're saying to me?"

Timothy sighed heavily. "I maybe overlooked the letter in my rush this morning."

Kayla nodded. "That I could believe."

"You know without the letter we can't begin to have a place at Briarwood Farms."

"I know." She'd heard Papa tell Mama that the letter was his assurance of a job as head trainer. The letter was his proof that Jason Wood had indeed hired him. Mama had taken great care of the letter for almost six months, and Kayla since then.

Kayla forced back a tinge of fear. "I'll check for the letter myself when it's not a bother to Hope Murphy."

"And when will that be? She doesn't like us underfoot."

"I know. Later she'll go visit Mrs. Grier like she does every morning when the babes are napping. I'll look then."

"And I hope you find it."

"I will find it!" Kayla touched the sack of food. "You know we must share this with the family. It hurts me to see them all hungry."

"I brought enough to share," he said quietly. "I knew you'd not be able to tuck away the food only for us." He rubbed a grimy hand over the carrots, then pulled two away from the bunch. "Save out these for us for later, will you?"

She nodded. "I'll tuck them in my bag." She touched the greens, then the long slender carrot that she knew would taste sweet and delicious.

Timothy jumped up with the sack in his hand and opened the door. "Hope Murphy, I brought something for your dinner," he sang out.

Kayla watched the look of pleasure on Hope's face as she looked in the bag. Suddenly she scowled.

"You didn't steal these, did you?" she asked sharply.

Timothy's face fell, then he lifted his head high. "I am an O'Brian, Hope Murphy, and I don't steal."

She flushed and turned away. "See that you never do." She smelled the onion, rubbed a carrot, and bit off the end of it and chewed it as if she was starving. Mary sat at her feet looking up at her, while Angel reached for the carrot. "When you have more teeth you can eat one, Angel. For you I'll cook some. For you and for Mary." Hope glanced over at four-year-old Sara, who was lost in her own world with her rag doll. Hope turned back to Timothy. "I must be thanking you for this, Timothy O'Brian."

"You are welcome."

Kayla knew it took a lot for Timothy to say that. She knew that he'd wanted to keep the food for them, but she also knew he could never eat fruit and vegetables when the others had only porridge, bread and lard, and potatoes boiled in their skins. At times Sean Murphy had apples, but there was never enough for the children.

Hope washed three carrots, dropped them in a sugar sack

22

along with an apple, and handed the sack to Timothy. "Run these to Sean. It will please him." Her face softened as it always did when she thought of Sean.

Suddenly the door burst open, and Glendon stood there gasping for breath. "Mama, come quick! Michael is hurt."

Hope sucked in her breath, and the color drained from her face.

Kayla touched her arm. "I'll go see to Michael. You sit down and rest."

"No! You stay with the babes and I'll see to Michael. Timothy, take the food to Sean." Hope ran after Glendon, her breath in short gasps.

Timothy whispered, "Kayla, check for the letter quick-like."

Kayla stepped around Mary and Angel and opened the bag that held the important papers and Mama's diary. Kayla looked over everything. An icy band clamped around her heart. The letter was indeed gone. Without the letter they couldn't find Briarwood Farms. She turned a stricken face to Timothy.

He nodded grimly.

She turned to Sara. "Did you open my bag and take anything out of it, Sara?"

Sara looked up from her doll, but the vacant look in her eyes made Kayla realize that she wouldn't get an answer.

"I will tell Sean Murphy it's gone," said Timothy gruffly. "He will learn the truth."

"Why would anyone take it? Or want it?" cried Kayla. "It must be in here!" Once again she looked through the papers, but the folded letter was not there. She touched Mama's diary, and her skin burned. She jerked her hand away and closed the bag.

"I'll be back before long," said Timothy.

Kayla nodded. Mary burst into tears and tugged on Kayla's dress. She picked up the crying baby and tried to soothe her as Timothy walked out the door.

Sara looked around, then slowly stood and walked to Kayla's bag. Kayla watched in alarm as Sara opened it and pulled out the diary. "Sara read to baby," Sara said.

"No, Sara," said Kayla gently. With Mary on her hip Kayla took the diary from Sara and stuck it back in the bag. "Sara, you must not touch my things."

"Sara read," said Sara, reaching for the diary.

Kayla set Mary on the floor, and she immediately burst into tears. Kayla closed the bag and held it out of Sara's reach. "You can't touch my things," she said sternly over Mary's wailing.

Angel leaned down to hug Mary and tipped themselves both over just as Hope walked in the door with a sobbing Michael in front of her. A cut above his eye dripped blood down his dirty face. Silently Duncan and Glendon followed them in. Hope scowled at Kayla on her way to the washbowl.

Flushing, Kayla set her bag down and picked up Mary and patted Angel's head. "How is Michael?"

"He'll live," snapped Hope. "But he'll be the death of me yet." He stopped crying as she gently wiped the blood from his forehead and face. "The cut's not too deep. You sit quietly a while with this rag on it and you'll be just fine in a bit." She sat Michael on a rolled mat, and he held the damp rag to his forehead. "Duncan, Glendon, go outdoors, but stay out of trouble."

They walked out and closed the door without slamming it.

Mary had stopped crying and lay with her head on Kayla's shoulder. Kayla took a deep breath. "Mrs. Murphy, I can't find my papa's letter from Briarwood Farms. 'Twas in my bag."

"Don't be bothering me about a letter," snapped Hope.

Kayla bit her lower lip and gently rocked Mary to sleep.

*H*er trembling hands locked behind her back, Kayla watched Hope Murphy walk down the street to visit Mrs. Grier just as she did each afternoon when Sara, Angel, and Mary napped. The warm wind whipped smells of the ocean through the air. Children ran and shouted in the street, stepping aside only for a wagon or buggy. All the immigrants up and down the street, Kayla included, had expected to walk on streets of gold and live in mansions in this place called America. She sighed heavily, then slowly stepped back inside. She had thought moving to America would be perfect. And it would've been if they could've gone right to Briarwood Farms.

"I must find the letter before she returns," whispered Kayla as she quietly closed the door. All morning Hope Murphy had kept her busy outdoors with the children. She glanced under the table where Sara, Angel, and Mary slept soundly on a mat where they wouldn't easily be stepped on. The three boys were playing outdoors with other noisy boys. Timothy had gone off to find any work that could be had in exchange for more food, but before he'd left he'd whispered to her, "Sean found a way for us to go to Briarwood Farms. We sail for Baltimore in two days. You must find the letter if it's to be found."

His words rang in Kayla's ears as she opened her bag and searched methodically for the letter. Perspiration dotted her face, and a chill ran down her spine. She wanted to pour out the contents of the bag and frantically rummage through it, but she couldn't take a chance on Hope Murphy returning or the babes awaking.

She touched Mama's diary, groaned, and picked it up. A picture of Mama filling a page with her careful script flashed across her mind. "Oh, Mama," she whispered brokenly, "I need you."

Kayla flipped through the pages of the diary, and it opened to a spot almost exactly in the middle. The letter was folded and stuck inside the diary.

Kayla gasped, lifted out the letter, and pushed the diary back into the bag. Who had put the letter inside the diary?

"Someone looked through our things," she whispered in alarm. It had to be one of the Murphys.

Hope Murphy?

Anger rushed through Kayla, and she pressed her lips into a straight, hard line, just as she'd seen Mama do in her anger. She had to find a place to put the letter, to put all her private papers and Mama's diary, so no prying eye could read them again. How dare anyone open their bag and read the papers inside!

She glanced down at Sara. Kayla narrowed her eyes. Maybe she was wrong about Hope Murphy. Maybe it had only been Sara wanting to read to her dolly.

Kayla nodded. That she could believe. The anger drained away as she glanced through the packed boxes to see where she could hide the papers out of Sara's reach.

"Mama's china dishes," whispered Kayla. She nodded and smiled. She'd hide them behind Mama's dishes. Even Hope Murphy made the babes stay away from that box.

Kayla glanced over the boxes, then looked again. She frowned. Where was the box of Mama's good china dishes that she'd packed and guarded herself?

Kayla bit her lower lip and forced back the panic. The box had to be here. Frantically she ran her hands over each box that belonged to her and Timothy. The box of china dishes wasn't there. She turned to look around the room in case Hope Murphy had moved it to a safer place. But there was no sign of the box in the tiny room.

"No, no, no," mouthed Kayla, shaking her head.

Would Timothy take them to sell or trade? Kayla shook her head harder. He'd never do that without talking to her first.

Had a thief stolen the dishes? But when would he have a chance? Someone was here at all times, or just outside the door.

Angry tears burned Kayla's eyes as she realized the terrible truth: Sean or Hope Murphy had taken Mama's china dishes. "Not Sean," Kayla whispered through a dry throat. "He's too honest to do such a deed. Hope Murphy did it. She did indeed. It must be her doing."

Her face flushed with anger, Kayla pushed the bag with the letter and diary down behind a box of Timothy's clothes. She flipped back her long dark hair, then tied it back in place with quick jerks.

How could she confront Hope Murphy with her suspicions? And what if she was wrong? What if Timothy had taken them? He had changed in the past few weeks, and the change wasn't good.

Her dress swishing around her ankles, she walked toward the door. Maybe Timothy would get back before Hope Murphy returned.

Sara flipped over in her sleep and lay half on and half off the mat. She didn't awake, so Kayla carefully eased open the door and stood on the step just outside. The noise and smells pressed in on her until she wanted to scream at the top of her lungs.

Just then Timothy walked into sight, his shoulders bent and his head down. He looked defeated and tired.

Another wave of anger washed over Kayla, and she clenched her fists at her sides. Life wasn't fair to Timothy! He was too young to have to face such hardship!

Suddenly he stopped. Kayla cocked her brow and watched him questioningly. She knew he hadn't seen her. As she watched, he squared his shoulders, lifted his head, and began whistling as he walked.

"Oh, Timothy," she muttered around a lump in her throat. She knew he didn't want her to see him discouraged. She waited, and when he saw her he waved and grinned as if he hadn't a care in the world.

When he stood beside her she said, "Did you find work?"

He hesitated, then shook his head. "I could lie and say I did, but an O'Brian does not lie!"

"No, an O'Brian does not lie." She rested her hands on his thin shoulders. "Timothy, did you take Mama's good china dishes?"

He frowned. "Take them?"

"To sell them for food."

He shook his head. "They're inside with all of our things."

"The box is gone, Timothy."

His muscles tightened, and anger leaped in his blue eyes. "'Tis her! She took them. I found her looking through them,

30

admiring them one day. She looked guilty and said she only wanted to touch them." He rubbed the sleeve of his soiled shirt. "She sold them, I'm sure."

"Oh, Timothy!"

"'Tis true!"

"I hate to believe it."

"You don't want to believe bad of anyone, Kayla, and you know it."

She sighed.

Timothy shoved his hands deep into the pockets of his pants. "I knew when she was looking at them that she meant to sell them. I knew when I saw Sean Murphy with new shoes and a warm coat that she had sold them. But I couldn't bring myself to look."

Kayla twisted her apron around her hand. "Why didn't you tell me, Timothy?"

"I didn't want to believe it myself." He dropped to the step and propped his elbows on his bony knees. "When first we moved in, she took the only money we had to keep us. She wanted Sean to think she was doing it out of the kindness of her heart."

"It is hard with a family this size, Timothy."

He scowled at her. "She took the money, and now she has taken the china dishes."

Kayla sank down beside Timothy. "What are we going to do?"

"Tell Sean."

"He'll be angry at her. I don't want that."

"I don't either, but she has no right to take our money or our dishes."

"Here she comes," whispered Kayla. She peeked inside the room to see the babes still asleep.

31

Timothy jumped up, his hands knotted at his sides.

Slowly Kayla stood. "Take care what you say, Timothy." She knew it wouldn't do any good to tell him to keep quiet. He was one to speak first and think later. She always *thought* first and often knew better than to speak.

Hope Murphy stopped in front of them, her face red from the walk, her breath short. She frowned slightly.

"Mrs. Murphy . . ." said Timothy sharply.

"Yes?"

Kayla held her breath.

Timothy stepped down beside Hope Murphy. He was almost as tall as she was. "Mama's good china dishes are gone."

Hope's face closed, and she lifted her chin slightly. "I sold them, and I had every right to. I can't take in you two orphans without money to feed you."

"But you didn't feed us with the money," said Kayla coldly.

Hope flushed. "That I didn't. But I will from the money Sean Murphy earns on the dock. He needed shoes and a coat. The babes needed winter clothes. Can you blame me for wanting to take care of my family?"

"You stole from us!" cried Timothy.

"Hush! I did no such thing." Hope glanced around to see if anyone had heard, but no one had.

"You did," snapped Kayla.

"I'll tell Sean," said Timothy coldly.

The color drained from Hope's face and she swayed, her hand at her heart. "No . . . No . . . Please don't tell him. He's a good man and 'twould break his heart."

"You should not have stolen the china dishes," whispered Kayla hoarsely. "They were Mama's!"

"I had no money," whispered Hope. "What could I do?"

Kayla sighed heavily as she gripped Timothy's arm to keep him from spewing out more anger. "What you've done, you've done. We can't stay angry, Mrs. Murphy."

"I can," snapped Timothy.

Hope hung her head. "I had to do it . . . For the money."

"Sean will see that we get back our china dishes," said Timothy.

Hope's eyes widened. "No! . . . Don't tell Sean."

"I will," said Timothy coldly.

"Let me tell him, so that he understands. Please, please, let *me* tell him."

Timothy pressed his lips tightly together, but Kayla said, "Tell him tonight. Tonight! Or *we* will."

"I will tell him," whispered Hope "Tonight." She shivered.

"He'll be ashamed of you for sure," said Timothy.

"I cannot bear it!" cried Hope with tears in her eyes.

Kayla tightened her grip on Timothy's arm. A wagon rolled past pulled by two gray draft horses. Kayla waited until the noise died away. "We'll be leaving in two days. Then you won't have to concern yourself with us or our things."

Hope gasped, her hand fluttering at the high collar of her faded dress. "And where will you be going?"

"To Maryland, of course," said Kayla.

"Sean found a man to take us there," said Timothy, pulling away from Kayla. "We would leave today if we could."

Kayla wanted to do just that, but she knew they'd have to sleep on the street if they did.

Hope tucked a strand of hair into the bun at the nape of her neck, retied her apron, and cleared her throat. "I have an errand for you both to run."

Frowning, Kayla studied Hope. She was suddenly acting

33

more nervous—and more guilty. "What errand, Mrs. Murphy?"

Just then Mary started crying, and Angel joined in. Sara picked up her rag doll and hugged it as she sucked her thumb.

Hope turned to the babes in relief. "I want you to take the little ones out for a breath of air. Walk them down the street and let them play under the tree next to the stables. But bring them back in time for supper."

Kayla wanted to refuse, but she pinned a dry nappy on Mary, handed her to Timothy, and walked out with Angel and Sara.

At the tree, while the babes played with the few leaves that had fallen, Kayla leaned close to Timothy. He still looked angry, and she wanted to see a smile on his face. "I found the letter, Timothy."

He sighed in relief. "So I was wrong. Do you have it with you?"

"No. It's in the bag, but I stuck the bag where Sara can't get at it. It'll be safe for two days."

"I'd feel a sight better if you had the letter on you."

Kayla nodded thoughtfully. Mama had often pinned important papers inside her dress. Kayla would do the same. "When we get back I'll pin the letter inside my dress, and there it'll stay until we need it at Briarwood Farms."

The whimpering Mary in her arms, Kayla stopped just inside the Murphys' door. Timothy, with the squirming Angel in his arms, was close behind her. A stranger sat at the table talking to Hope Murphy. Circles of red dotted her cheeks as she pushed a paper across the table to the man. The smell of roast beef filled the room. A shiver trickled down Kayla's back as the man folded the paper and stuck it in his inside pocket. Kayla bit her lower lip. Something terrible was going to happen, she was sure of it. *Thank You, Father in Heaven, for watching out for us,* she prayed silently.

"Kayla, let's get out of here," whispered Timothy urgently. He stood Angel on the floor and stepped back.

Kayla sat Mary beside Angel and clutched Timothy's hand.

"Wait!" cried Hope, reaching out to them. Her hand trembled, and she quickly hid it in her lap. "This . . . this man came to help . . . you. He's going to take you to your new . . . home."

The man pushed himself up, his bowler in his hand. As tall as Sean Murphy, but rail-thin, he was dressed in a suit as dark as his soft brown eyes. A warm smile spread across his narrow face as he looked from Kayla to Timothy. "I'm Tom Drake. You have nothing to fear from me. I've come to help you leave this city and get to wide open places where you can make something of yourselves."

"I don't trust him," whispered Timothy for Kayla's ears alone.

She wanted to reassure Timothy, but she didn't trust him either. "We have made something of ourselves, sir. We're O'Brians!"

"And proud of it, so it seems." Mr. Drake set his hat on the table. "But I'm sure you want to move out of the city and into the country."

Sara tugged on Mr. Drake's sleeve, and he bent down to her. She held up her rag doll. Mr. Drake kissed Sara's cheek, then kissed the doll.

"You've a fine doll there," he said.

Sara smiled and hugged her doll to her.

Suddenly Kayla trusted the man because of his actions. Kayla looked Tom Drake square in the eyes. "Why is it you want to help us? We have nothing to give you in return."

"Nothing at all!" said Timothy with his fists clenched at his sides.

Mr. Drake chuckled softly. "I don't expect anything. It's my job to help children."

"Mr. Drake wants you to go with him . . . now," said Hope, her face flushed as she stood behind her chair, gripping the back of it.

"Go where?" asked Timothy sharply.

"Don't be frightened," said Mr. Drake. "I'm taking you to a place closer to the dock, so that when the ship's ready to sail you can walk right on it without delaying departure."

Her blue eyes sparkling, Kayla turned to Timothy. "Did you hear that, Timothy? We have nothing to fear. We'll go with Mr. Drake."

Timothy hesitated, then shrugged. "I'll have to find a way to get all of our things there."

"I'll see to that," said Hope.

"What about Mama's china dishes?" asked Timothy, scowling at Hope.

"I'll take care of that too," she said stiffly.

"You may each bring a portmanteau with your clothes," said Mr. Drake. "We must be on our way."

Kayla nodded at Timothy, then smiled at Mr. Drake. "We will be ready to leave in a shake of a lamb's tail." She walked to the pile of boxes. Mr. Drake talked to Sara and Angel, and Hope took care of Mary. Kayla found the case with the clothes that once had been Mama's but were now hers, and pushed them into the bag that held papers, the letter, Mama's diary, a Bible, and Mama's favorite book of verse. She buckled it shut and turned with it in her hand just as Timothy buckled his shut.

"We're ready," he said. He wouldn't look at Hope Murphy.

"Good-bye, children," said Hope with a false-sounding warmth in her voice. "I am glad that we could help you as much as we did. I wanted to do more, but what could I do what with six babes and another on the way?"

"Good-bye," said Kayla. She bent down to the little girls, kissed their cheeks, then smiled stiffly at Hope.

"I'll tell Sean good-bye for you," said Hope.

"We'll tell him ourselves at the dock," said Timothy.

Hope started to speak, then closed her mouth and nodded.

"Let's be off," said Mr. Drake, twirling his bowler on his finger to make Sara giggle. "I want you settled in before dark."

"You'll find this is for the best," said Hope as they walked out her door.

Icy chills ran along Kayla's spine. What did Hope mean by that?

Timothy stopped and stared back at Hope, then turned and walked ahead of Mr. Drake and Kayla down the step and onto the noisy street.

"Where are you going, Timothy?" called Duncan Murphy from the street where he was playing with other boys.

"To our new home," said Timothy brightly. "You boys be good."

"Good-bye," said Kayla, waving to the boys. She was going to miss them. "Help your mama take care of the babes."

Kayla walked down the brick street without speaking, excitement bubbling up inside her. Finally they were going to Briarwood Farms! She watched the stiff way Timothy walked. Why wasn't he excited too? She glanced up at Mr. Drake beside her. He looked deep in thought, his face in shadows from his bowler. He caught her look and smiled. She smiled, then looked down at the toes of her worn shoes — Mama's shoes that finally fit her. She walked a little faster.

Smells of the livery and the ocean mixed with the smoke from chimneys. Kayla watched a fine buggy carrying a well-dressed man and woman drive past, the team of matched bays stepping proudly. She saw Timothy look at the bays with admiration, and she knew she'd been right to judge the horses as exceptional.

Mr. Drake said, "I see you like horses."

"Yes. We can't wait to train them," Timothy answered politely.

"You'll probably get the chance." He went into a long account of a sorrel that he'd had years before that had obeyed his every command almost before he gave it. "Never had a horse I liked better. The one I have now barely picks up his feet when he walks."

"Timothy and I would be glad to check him over for you," said Kayla with a flash of interest in her eyes.

"That's kind of you, but I don't believe there'll be a chance. You're leaving tomorrow."

"Tomorrow?" Kayla's heart leaped. "Timothy, did you hear that? Tomorrow we go!"

Timothy whirled around, his eyes thoughtful. "Tomorrow? You're not mistaken?"

"Not at all. I should know." Mr. Drake brushed soot off his sleeve. "I've been working on this a long time."

Kayla chuckled under her breath. Wind blew a strand of her long raven hair across her flushed cheek. She hooked it behind her ear and wished she could retie the string that held her hair from flying over her face and shoulders. She frowned down at her dirty, faded dress. She should've taken time to change.

A few minutes later they reached the docks. Kayla looked around for Sean Murphy, but didn't see him. She took in the confusion of drays and carts, wheelbarrows and barrels. The ships' gilded figureheads, with jib booms thrust over the cobbled streets, swayed lazily with the roll of the water. A well-seasoned paddle-wheeler was tied further down the dock, a crowd of ragged children looking at it. Commercial merchants bargained with peddlers. Land speculators talked with traders. Gangs of sweating, tight-muscled men carried heavy barrels up the gangplank, shouting curses if anyone stepped in the way.

"I'm going to find Sean Murphy," shouted Timothy in order to be heard over the racket.

"No!" Mr. Drake leaped forward and caught Timothy's arm. "Stay with me . . . I don't want you to get lost."

Timothy jerked free. "I won't get lost! I'm not a babe!"

"We've been here many times," said Kayla.

"We're going over there to get the other children," said Mr. Drake. "I want you both to stay with me."

"Are all those children going to Baltimore?" asked Kayla in surprise.

"Baltimore?" Mr. Drake lifted a dark brow. "Albany, you mean."

"Do we have to go to Albany to get to Baltimore?" asked Timothy.

"We're not going to Baltimore," said Mr. Drake. "We're going to Albany to catch the train west."

"And will that take us to Briarwood Farms?" asked Kayla.

"It'll take us to a lot of farms," said Mr. Drake brightly. "Farms with horses to tend."

Kayla looked uneasily at Timothy. She could tell he felt the same as she did. She turned back to Mr. Drake. "Are you taking us to Maryland . . . to Briarwood Farms?"

Mr. Drake frowned. "Where did you get that idea? I'm taking all of you children on the train. We're going west where you'll find families to adopt you."

Kayla stumbled back and almost fell over a coil of rope. "Who are you?" asked Kayla in a strangled voice.

"I'm Tom Drake with the Children's Aid Society, of course. You know that. Mrs. Murphy said you were more than willing to go with us since she couldn't take care of you."

Kayla shook her head, her eyes wide in alarm.

Timothy grabbed Kayla's hand and cried, "Let's go!"

"You're not going anywhere!" snapped Mr. Drake. "I have papers signed here in my pocket that put me in charge of you. You have to go where I say. You can't run the streets of New York City!"

Kayla gripped her case with one hand and Timothy's hand with the other. She would not let anyone take her on the train west when she was supposed to go to Maryland!

Suddenly a barrel rolled down the gangplank toward them. Someone shouted, and people scrambled out of the way. Kayla and Timothy used the moment of confusion to slip away from Mr. Drake, ran around a stack of boxes and out of his sight, then dodged around barrels and a crowd of men. The case grew heavy in Kayla's hand, but she couldn't drop it. All her personal belongings were inside the case, along with the letter from Briarwood Farms. The smells around her sickened her. The string slipped from her hair, and the wind tangled it around her slender shoulders. She stubbed her toe on a plank and almost fell.

Several minutes later she ducked between two large wooden crates with Timothy just ahead of her. She dropped her case as pain shot through her. Gasping for breath, she held her side. Timothy bent over, panting. Fear pricked her skin as she huddled behind him.

Would Mr. Drake find them and force them to go with him?

"I think we lost him," whispered Timothy raggedly.

Just then a hand grabbed Kayla's tangled hair and tugged on her hard. She cried out in pain and in fear.

5

Kayla screamed again as she twisted around to see who had grabbed her by the hair. She caught a glimpse of fine fawn pants and black polished boots.

"Thought you could hide from me, did you, girl?" snarled her captor. He released her hair, only to grip her arm even more tightly.

She looked at him, her eyes wide with fear. From his speech she knew he was English. He was a few inches taller than she, not more than thirty years old, and well-dressed with a nicely trimmed beard. His blue eyes were as hard as ice. "What do you want with me?" she cried.

"Let her go!" shouted Timothy.

"Get away from here, sonny. It's me and the girl who have business." The man flipped Kayla's hair out of her face. "I'd know you anywhere with that mass of black hair, you Irish wench. Changing your clothes didn't help at all. You're coming with me. You run away again and it'll be prison for you. Rotting prison with rats, maniacs, and food — what there is of it — full of bugs."

"Let her go!" cried Timothy again, jabbing the man with his fists.

"Get away from here, boy!" The man backhanded Timothy, sending him sprawling to the dock. "This is between the girl and me."

"Timothy!" cried Kayla, struggling to break free. She kicked, but missed the man's leg.

"Quiet yourself, girl!" The man circled her waist and clamped a hard hand over her mouth.

Timothy leaped up and charged the man, but he caught Timothy with a blow on the chin that sent him flying back to land in an unconscious heap beside Kayla's case.

"Timothy!" screamed Kayla, squirming, kicking, clawing.

"You stop the noise or I'll haul you off to prison this very minute!"

Whimpering, Kayla clamped her mouth closed. Was the man crazy?

He pulled her arms behind her and tied her wrists securely with a piece of rope that he cut from a box, then forced her to walk with him away from the crates, and away from Timothy still unconscious near her case. "I didn't buy you to have you run every chance you get, girl. Twice you've run in a week."

"You did not buy me!"

"As good as," he snapped. "I paid your passage over, and you're indentured to me for the next three and a half years."

"No! I am Kayla O'Brian! I've never set eyes on you before!" She screamed and jerked away. She staggered and almost fell, but he caught her and jerked her to him. She screamed again, looking helplessly around. Why wouldn't anyone notice what was happening to her? How could they keep working as if nothing was going on? She caught the eye of a big dockworker. "Help me," she mouthed.

He stepped forward, an angry scowl on his beefy face. "What's going on here?"

Kayla's captor glared at the dockworker. "This is none of your concern."

"He's kidnapping me, and he knocked out my brother!" cried Kayla. "Help me!"

The dockworker growled low in his throat. "Let the girl go."

Kayla's captor narrowed his eyes into slits of steel. "Don't interfere in this."

"Unhand the girl!" The dockworker doubled his fists, and his huge arm and shoulder muscles moved under his stained shirt.

"Go back to your own business! I'm Warton Tweed, and this girl belongs to me. I have the papers to prove it."

"That he does not!" cried Kayla.

The dockworker hesitated. "Show me the papers." He couldn't read, but he knew the man wouldn't know that.

Impatiently Warton Tweed pulled papers from the inside of his suit coat and held them out to the dockworker. "Signed with her own X," said Warton Tweed testily.

"That is not my X," cried Kayla. "I can sign my name. I can read and write!"

The dockworker looked at the papers without taking them from Warton Tweed. "She might be yours, but you don't have to manhandle her."

"She's a runaway."

"No, I'm not!"

The dockworker shrugged and walked back to the stack of crates.

Kayla sagged in defeat. "I am Kayla O'Brian," she said weakly.

"You're Megan, and we both know it."

At the name she slumped against him, the very life drained from her body. Mama's name was Megan.

The man chuckled drily. "So the game is over, is it? All the fight is gone, and you're ready to return with me." He caught her elbow and tugged her along beside him away from the dock, the smells, the noise, the confusion and to a crimson-seated buggy pulled by a team of white horses. He lifted her in, then sat beside her, unwrapped the reins, and slapped them against the horses. They stepped lively, pulling the buggy at a steady pace.

Kayla leaned away from Warton Tweed. "Let me go. Please don't do this! I am Kayla O'Brian!"

"You either close your mouth or I'll stick a gag in it," snapped Warton Tweed.

She bit her lower lip, but didn't speak.

"That's better."

She strained to look back to see if there was any sign of Timothy. There wasn't, and tears flooded her eyes. How would he find her? How would she get free and find him? What would happen to him in this dangerous city? What would happen to her?

"Tears, I see. It won't do you any good."

"Please, sir, I am truly Kayla O'Brian."

"I'd untie your hands, Megan, but you might jump out and run away again."

"I am not . . . not . . ." She couldn't bring herself to say the name.

"Mrs. Tweed has been asking about you."

"Mrs. Tweed?" Surely his wife could see that he'd brought home the wrong person.

"Mrs. Tweed . . . My wife. She arrived home today after a visit with her mother."

Kayla closed her eyes tightly. Defeated again!

"But I already told you that."

"You did not!"

He sighed heavily. "Just before you ran. You're a stubborn piece of baggage."

She sniffed and blinked to clear the tears from her eyes. "Why won't you believe me? I'm Kayla O'Brian! I am!"

He slowed the team, then turned down a tree-lined street. Grand homes stood back from the street. Each home had at least an acre of front lawn with flowers still in bloom and leafy green trees, with a few just turning their fall colors. Kayla perked up. She and Timothy had walked past these very homes only a few days ago. If she could get away she could run back to the docks to find Timothy. She tensed to leap, then knew she couldn't do it safely with her hands tied behind her. She'd have to wait until he set her free.

Warton Tweed tipped his hat to a passing buggy. "That was Bracken Loftus and his wife and son. You should be thankful he didn't buy your papers. He beats his servants."

Kayla shuddered.

"I have a temper, as you very well know, but I would never beat a servant."

"You struck Timothy!"

Warton Tweed scowled at her. "Timothy?"

"My brother! He was trying to protect me, and you knocked him down. Maybe killed him!"

"You have no family. It's on your papers."

She groaned. Why did he insist that she was someone else? Why wouldn't he believe her?

He slapped the reins, and the team trotted, their hooves clip-clopping on the brick street. "Mrs. Tweed has no one to fix her hair. And with the party tonight she needs your help with her toilet. You'll serve as well. You are to wear the pink and white uniform that Bertha laid in your room. It will look a sight better than the oversized rag you're wearing now."

Kayla looked down at her dress. When first she'd started wearing it, it had fit better, but she'd dropped in weight until now it hung on her. It was indeed dirty and faded with a fresh rip at the gathered waist.

He turned down another street and finally drove up beside a brick mansion with a wide clipped lawn and bright flowers and shrubs galore. Several chimneys reached up into the gray sky. Bright curtains hung at the windows. The beauty of it all took Kayla's breath away. She glanced at Warton Tweed. He must indeed be a very wealthy man.

An old black man with snow-white hair ran up to take the team to the stable.

Kayla tried to catch his eye to beg for help, but he wouldn't look at her.

Warton Tweed stepped down from the buggy, then easily lifted Kayla down to stand her beside him. "I'm going to untie your hands so we don't upset Mrs Tweed, but if you try to run again I will indeed escort you directly to prison."

Kayla trembled. She knew he meant what he said. Just the thought of prison frightened her. One of the street boys had told of his mother who'd been put in prison for stealing. When she was released six months later, she looked at her own son with vacant eyes. She smelled like a chamber pot that hadn't been emptied for weeks, and her clothes were slashed to ribbons. She couldn't speak and sat all day in their room picking lice from her matted hair.

Her legs weak, Kayla walked beside Warton Tweed to the wide door. He untied her hands, and she rubbed her wrists, wincing at the pain. "Please listen to me," she whispered hoarsely, her blue eyes wide with pleading as she looked into his eyes. "I am Kayla O'Brian. I came with my family from County Offaly."

"Then where is your family?" he asked coldly as he stood beside the closed front door, his hands resting lightly on his hips.

She couldn't find words, but finally she forced out, "My brother Timothy is back at the docks. You knocked him out."

"That boy was a street urchin, nothing more. Now, no more nonsense." He unlocked the door and pulled Kayla inside with him.

She dropped her chin to her chest and closed her eyes to hold back the hot tears.

Kayla's knees buckled and she would've crashed to the slate floor, but Warton Tweed caught her and held her up.

"I'll get you to the kitchen and you're going to eat so you'll have strength for the party. It's only three hours away. You must bathe and change quickly so you can help Mrs. Tweed." He pulled a cord that rang a bell deeper in the house. "Amee will see to you." At the sound of footsteps he leaned close to her ear. "Don't run away again."

A girl about Kayla's age stopped in front of Warton Tweed with a slight curtsy. She had light-brown hair, pinned back, and wore a small white and pink cap and a pink and white dress that just brushed the floor. She glanced quickly at Kayla, then back to Warton Tweed. "Good evening, Mr. Tweed. What can I do for you?"

"Amee, take Megan to the kitchen, see that she eats, then get her upstairs to bathe and change. Make sure she does something with this hair." He flicked Kayla's tangled mass of black hair. "She must look presentable for the party tonight."

"I'll take care of her, Mr. Tweed." Amee smiled at Kayla,

but Kayla couldn't make her frozen mouth smile. "Come with me, Megan."

Kayla hesitated.

"Go with her," said Mr. Tweed sternly. "Amee, I'll be upstairs with Mrs. Tweed. Send Megan to help with Mrs. Tweed's hair."

Kayla reluctantly walked with Amee across the great hall. She glanced back to see Mr. Tweed running up the wide stairs, two steps at a time. She turned back to Amee and whispered, "Do you know me?"

Amee frowned slightly, then grinned. "Should I? I only started to work here this morning. Just after you ran away, I heard." Amee stopped and studied Kayla. "Why do you want to leave this place? I've dreamed of working in such a place ever since I left Massachusetts. The pay is good, and we have a whole attic just for servants. The last place I worked didn't have servant's quarters, and I had to sleep in the pantry on the floor."

"Amee, I am not . . . not . . ." Kayla couldn't bring herself to say the name. "I'm Kayla O'Brian. Mr. Tweed thinks I'm . . . I'm . . . someone else."

"Are you sure you're not weak in the head from hunger?"

"I am hungry, but I know what I know." Kayla rubbed her bruised wrists. "You must help me, Amee! Help me get back to my brother."

Amee opened her brown eyes wide and pressed her work-roughened hand to her throat. "I couldn't do that, miss. No! You must stay here. I heard Mr. Tweed's anger when you ran, and I know he'd have you tossed in the Black Hole if you leave again. I wouldn't want my worst enemy put in that prison." She shuddered. "No . . . I won't help you get away no matter how much you beg."

"I must escape!" Kayla looked around wildly. The hallway stretched on and on, with doors opening on either side of it.

"You are coming with me to the kitchen. After you've eaten and are cleaned up, then you can think clearer." Amee tugged on Kayla's sleeve. "Come on . . . We don't have much time."

With a ragged sigh Kayla let Amee lead her to the vast kitchen, where a tall, thin woman worked over a hot cook stove covered with pots and pans. Smells of vegetables, gravy, lamb, and fresh bread filled the room, making Kayla's mouth water and her stomach growl. It had been a long time since she'd eaten such food.

"Wash there and sit down." Amee pushed Kayla toward a heavy oak chair at the long oak table. "Gretchen, this is Megan."

The woman at the stove turned with a lifted brow. "Sit and eat," she said in a voice so deep it could've been a man's. A big white cap covered most of her gray hair. Wrinkles lined her thin face. "So you're the one always running. I saw you a couple of times. I trust you're ready to stay put this time and work like you should."

Kayla sagged against the table. She couldn't find the energy to tell anyone else who she really was.

Amee set a tall glass of cold milk and a plate heaped with hot food and two thick slices of bread covered with fresh butter in front of Kayla. "Now eat . . . I'll carry hot water to the tub for you."

Kayla picked up the fork and lifted a bite of orange carrots dripping with butter to her mouth. Slowly she dropped it back to the plate. Never in her life had she eaten a meal without first thanking God for it. What was happening to her? Had all the terrible things made her forget about her Heavenly

Father? She locked her hands in her lap and bowed her head over the food. The smells made her weak as she silently thanked God for the food. "And take care of my Timothy. In Jesus' name, Amen," she whispered.

Thinking of Timothy almost stole her appetite away, but she picked up her fork and slowly ate every bite on her plate and drank the last drop of milk. For the first time in a long time she was comfortably full. It felt strange.

"Good girl," said Amee, patting Kayla's shoulder. "Now come with me and we'll get you cleaned up. Your bath is ready." Amee led her up two flights of narrow wooden stairs to a small room that held a tin tub almost full of water. "This will be the last time I carry your water for you, Megan." Amee smiled. "I might be nice, but there are things I refuse to do. One of them is wait hand and foot on another servant." She giggled. "Do I sound mean?"

"No. I wish you'd call me Kayla though."

Amee sighed. "I could call you Kayla when we're alone just to make you feel better, but in front of the others I must call you by your name . . . Megan."

Kayla slowly pulled off her shoes, stockings, dress, and underclothes. She slipped down in the tub, and the soothing water closed over her. Not since she'd left Ireland had she sat in a tub. Oh, it was wonderful!

"I'll wash your hair for you since we must hurry you along," said Amee. "I don't mind doing that at all. Once it's clean and brushed it'll be beautiful. I always wanted hair the color of a crow's wing, but I had to settle for this mouse-brown." She chattered away as she poured water over Kayla's head, rubbed in soap, and rinsed it out. "How old are you, Megan? Sorry." Amee giggled. "Kayla."

"Fourteen. You?"

"Fifteen. I've been working out since I was eleven."

"I've never worked out," said Kayla. "I worked at home back in County Offaly. Worked with horses and with the garden and in the house." Tears welled up in her eyes. She couldn't let herself think about her past. She had to look to the future. "Timothy, my brother and I, are on our way to Briarwood Farms in Maryland to work with horses there. We're to leave day after tomorrow." She turned with a splash and looked up at Amee. "I have to get to the ship so we can get to Maryland. I must!"

"Here's a towel. Step out and dry off and I'll help you with your hair. But I don't want to hear any more crazy talk."

With quick, sharp movements Kayla wrapped one towel around her head and dried off with another, letting Amee chatter about places where she'd worked. Kayla bit back a moan. Would she ever find anyone who would believe her and help her?

"Mrs. Tweed will be needing you soon, Kayla. She wanted me to do her hair, but I'm not good with hair. Oh, I can dry it and pin it back in a simple style or braid it, but I can't dress it high like Mrs. Tweed wants."

"I can. Hope Murphy showed me how." Anger at Hope rose inside Kayla and almost took her breath away. She jerked on the underclothes that were laid out for her, the pink and white uniform, and the white stockings and black shoes.

"Oh, Kayla, don't you look the beauty all dressed in clean, nice clothes! I wouldn't think you were the same girl."

"Thank you." She felt clean and refreshed. She knew that she'd have to bide her time and run away when she wouldn't be missed.

Amee sat her on a straight-back chair and carefully rubbed her hair dry with a thick towel. "I can clean, and I can greet people and make them feel welcome, but I can't manage hair." Quickly she braided Kayla's long, black hair into one long braid and pinned it in a circle on the back of her head, then pinned her white and pink cap in place. "You have beautiful cheekbones, and such a nice nose. Mine is too wide and almost flat. But I have nice lips, don't you think?"

Kayla looked at Amee's lips and nodded. Kayla had never taken much notice of her own appearance except to be clean and neat, until even that was impossible to do on board ship and later at the Murphys'. The thought of Hope Murphy sent a rush of fresh anger through her. How could Mrs. Murphy turn them over to the Children's Aid Society? She knew they were going to Maryland. Why had she done such a terrible, terrible thing?

"Let s get to work, Megan." Amee giggled and jabbed Kayla's arm playfully. "Kayla, I mean. Don't get mad at me if I forget to call you Kayla, will you?"

Kayla felt Amee's kindness, and she managed a smile. "I won't. But my name *is* Kayla O'Brian. And I can prove it as soon as I find my brother and our things. I have a Bible with my name and birth date."

"You do? We had a Bible at home too. Sometimes my grandma read it, but nobody else bothered." Amee talked all the way down the first flight of stairs and along the hall to Mrs. Tweed's room. She knocked and waited until a soft voice said to come in. Amee opened the door and pushed Kayla inside. Then Amee ran lightly away.

Kayla stood just inside the door of the huge bedroom. An intricately carved mahogany fireplace lined one wall. A four-poster bed that was so high it had two steps leading up to it stood out from another wall. High windows flanked the bed and were covered with rich burgundy drapes that matched the carpet. A girl sat at a dressing table with a big looking glass on the wall behind it. She turned to Kayla and smiled. She looked like a frightened doe.

"Hello," she said softly.

"Hello." Kayla stepped forward. "I'm Kayla O'Brian. Where is Mrs. Tweed? I'm supposed to do her hair."

The girl laughed. "*I* am Mrs. Tweed."

"You? You're but a girl!"

She laughed. "I'm Priscilla Tweed." She looked around as if she were making sure no one else could hear. "Sometimes it surprises me. I am seventeen. I've been married a month to Mr. Tweed." She looked around again, then slowly stood. "He was married before, but his wife died leaving him with two children. Papa arranged for me to marry him, but I find it isn't as bad as I thought it would be."

Kayla caught Mrs. Tweed's hand. "Please, will you help me?"

Priscilla frowned. "Help you? But you're here to help me. With my hair. Isn't it a sight?" She touched her long blonde hair. "I must look my best for a party we're giving tonight. My first party as the hostess. Oh, I wish Mama was here! I begged her to return with me, but she has four children at home who need her attention."

"I'm sure you'll do just fine." Kayla began to slowly brush Priscilla's long blonde hair as Priscilla went into great detail about her younger brothers and sisters. Carefully Kayla piled Priscilla's hair high and pinned it in place with tortoise-shell hairpins. She left a thick strand hanging down over her right shoulder and feathered out a few short strands at her temples. "You have beautiful hair."

Priscilla leaned toward the looking glass. "Oh, I am beautiful! I really am! I knew you'd be able to fix my hair!

Someone, maybe it was Thelma, said you had a way with hair."

Kayla's heart stopped. "Does Thelma know me?"

"But of course. She's been working here for weeks, and she trained you."

"Could I see her?"

"She's gone tonight. But she'll be back next week. You can see her then."

Kayla pushed back the wail of anguish that rose in her throat. "Is there anything else I can do for you?"

"I suppose not, Megan. But I am rather nervous about tonight. You don't happen to know how to pray, do you?"

Startled, Kayla stepped back. "Why do you ask?"

"I need more strength for tonight than I have. Mama says that God is my strength, but I always let her do the praying . . . Only she's not here." Priscilla sighed and fanned her suddenly flushed cheeks. "Amee says she doesn't pray. Thelma does, but she's not here either."

"I pray," said Kayla in a low voice. Could she pray for Priscilla Tweed when anger and frustration were so strong inside her?

"Will you pray for me? Please, Megan?" Her eyes full of fear, Priscilla gripped Kayla's hands tightly.

Finally Kayla bowed her head. "Heavenly Father, thank You for Your great love for us. You are indeed our strength. In Jesus' name I speak peace to Mrs. Tweed's heart. Help her to rely on Your strength tonight. Help her to smile and say the right things and to enjoy her party. Amen."

Impulsively Priscilla hugged Kayla, then stepped back and smiled. "Thank you. If there is ever anything I can do for you, just tell me."

"You could help me get away from here to find my brother."

"Oh my, no! Don't even say that!" Priscilla playfully slapped Kayla's arm. "But you're teasing with me, aren't you? I know you are. Now go downstairs and help serve."

Kayla nodded and slowly walked out the door.

Kayla crept down the hall to the back stairs. She sank to the top step and covered her face with her trembling hands. How could she survive tonight?

God is your strength.

The words rose up on the inside of her, and she lifted her head. "Yes!" she whispered. "God *is* my strength! Thank You, Father. Forgive me for feeling sorry for myself and for being angry."

Often Papa had said that when the Devil did something to cause them harm, they could turn it around by doing something to glorify God. "Do all that you do as if you're doing it for Jesus. Never, never let Satan defeat you. No attack from Satan can defeat you unless you allow it to. Ever since you let Jesus into your life, you are a child of the King! You are more than a conqueror through Jesus Christ our Lord. You can do all things through Christ who gives you strength." The words that Papa had said many times rang inside her, filled her, and pushed away her fear and anger and frustration.

"While I am here I will work for the Tweeds as if I'm

working for Jesus Himself, and somehow I'll get back to Timothy. That I will!"

A light of victory flashed in her eyes as she walked back downstairs to find Amee.

"My but you look chipper," said Amee with a grin. "The food and the bath brought you back to life."

Kayla smiled and shook her head. "No. 'Twas Jesus who did. He will work a miracle for me and help me get back to Timothy."

Amee cocked her head with interest. "Do you really believe in miracles?"

"That I do!"

"So did my grandma."

"So can you, Amee, if you put your trust in God and not in yourself."

"I've thought about it." Amee giggled and flung her hands wide. "We're getting a mite too serious here, Megan. We have a party to serve. You go out and greet the guests, and I'll take their wraps to the cloakroom." She walked toward the front door, then stopped and turned back to Kayla. "Don't you let Mr. Tweed hear you talking about getting out of here."

Kayla nodded. Somehow she had to prove to Mr. Tweed who she really was so he would let her go.

Just as she reached the wide front door the bell rang. She opened it, smiled, and ushered in the first guests. She recognized them as Mr. and Mrs. Bracken Loftus. He was the man Mr. Tweed had said beat his servants. He was smiling and relaxed and didn't seem at all the type.

"Mr. and Mrs. Tweed are expecting you," said Kayla as she motioned for them to walk to the front room, a huge room full of sofas and chairs, pieces of art, and a fireplace even more elaborate than the one in the master bedroom.

Amee took the cloaks and hat and carried them away while the Loftuses walked to join the Tweeds, who stood in the wide doorway of the front room. The heavy pocket doors were pushed inside the walls, and lamps and candles lit the room.

Before they reached the front-room doorway, the bell rang again and several more guests waited to enter. Cool air rushed in with them, along with different scents that the women wore. Kayla smiled and greeted each one. After a while she felt as if her smile was locked in place.

Talking and laughter drifted out from the front room. Soon it would be time for them to sit around the long dining room table and eat the delicious meal that Gretchen had cooked.

"Just two more and they'll all be here," whispered Amee as she once again stood waiting with Kayla. "Twenty-eight guests, but it seems more like a hundred, doesn't it?"

The bell rang, and once again Kayla swung the door wide. A man and woman stood there. The man was medium height, lean and muscled, with gray hair, hazel eyes, and a bruise on the side of his head. Kayla gasped. It was the man from the alley who'd almost run them down with his roan!

"My miracle!" she whispered. She reached out to him, but he pulled back, his eyes cold. "Sir, 'tis you! Would you help me, sir?"

Amee tugged on Kayla's arm. "Megan, what are you doing? Let them enter!"

"In the alley, sir . . . I helped you."

"Megan!" Amee tugged harder.

Kayla stepped out of the doorway, and the man and woman walked inside. "Forgive me, sir," said Kayla just above a whisper. "But I know who you are, and you know me. You must help me."

"What is she talking about, Andrew?" asked the woman, scowling at her husband.

"I'm sure I don't know, Belle." He wouldn't look at Kayla.

"But you know me!" cried Kayla. "Look at me!"

Amee jabbed Kayla's side. "Stop it," she hissed. "You're disturbing the party."

Kayla opened her mouth to say more, but closed it when she saw the anger on the woman's face and the fear in the man's eyes.

"Come this way," said Amee to the couple. She frowned over her shoulder at Kayla, then smiled at the man and woman. "Forgive Megan. She's had a hard day. But she'll be all right."

"She's a strange girl," muttered the woman.

"Very strange," said the man stiffly.

Kayla leaned weakly against the door. Somehow she had to make the man tell Mr. Tweed who she really was. Surely he'd listen to his own guest.

Just then Amee caught Kayla's arm and tugged her out of sight in the cloakroom. "What were you doing? You are a servant! You can't treat a guest that way!" She flung out her arms. "Oh, what am I going to do with you?"

"You must listen to me, Amee!" Kayla locked her icy hands in front of her. "That man knows me. But a few days ago he almost ran over Timothy and me when he galloped down an alley on his great roan. I saved him from two street boys who tried to rob him, maybe kill him."

Amee frowned and shook her head. "You're daft."

"I am not!" Tears filled Kayla's eyes. "I speak the truth! An O'Brian does not lie!"

"Don't try to speak to that man while he is here in this house as a guest or you'll embarrass the Tweeds, the man, and

64

yourself. You are a servant, and you must conduct yourself as one."

Kayla brushed the tears from her eyes and squared her shoulders. "I will not be embarrassing anyone. But I will get back to my Timothy. That I am sure of!"

Later Kayla took a deep breath to steady herself, then walked into the dining room full of people, talking and laughing quietly. Kayla set the tray of food on the sideboard, then picked up the bowl of cooked carrots while Amee carried the green beans. Kayla glanced around the table until she spotted the man she'd saved. During the course of the evening she'd learned he was Andrew Clements, a banker and land speculator. She caught his eye, but he looked quickly away. Why wouldn't he admit to knowing her? She caught a glimpse of her reflection in a narrow looking glass on the wall between two sconces filled with lit candles. She was clean, neat, and nice looking. When he'd seen her she had been dirty, ragged, and her hair a tangled mass. Perhaps he really didn't know who she was.

Quietly she walked around the table and spooned carrots onto the plates while Amee followed her with the beans. When she reached Andrew Clements she felt him stiffen, but she didn't speak or make any untoward movement. Later she'd find a way to speak to him privately. She'd help him remember her; then for sure he would help her convince Mr. Tweed that she was Kayla O'Brian.

She served Priscilla Tweed, who looked strained and tired. Kayla leaned close and whispered for her ears alone, "God is your strength."

Priscilla smiled and sat straighter. "Thank you, Megan," she said softly.

Several minutes later the last of the meal was served, with

dessert and coffee to come later. Kayla stood next to the side-board, waiting to take food or drink to anyone who wanted it. Forks clinked against china plates. Mr. Tweed said something that made the woman on his left laugh.

Kayla's feet ached by the end of the party. The shoes that had been provided for Megan were a little small for her. While Priscilla played the piano and sang for everyone, Kayla looked around the room for Andrew Clements. She didn't see him anywhere. His wife sat on the sofa with two other women. Kayla smiled and slipped out of the room. Now was her chance. She'd find Mr. Clements and speak to him privately.

She looked in the library, Mr. Tweed's study, the morning room, the front room, and all the other rooms on the first floor. Where was he? He wouldn't wander upstairs, would he?

Just then she caught a glimpse of a shadow out the glass doors off the morning room. She peeked out and saw that it was Mr. Clements, and he was alone. She smiled.

She slipped out. She smelled the chimney smoke in the air and heard the moan of a ship's horn. "Mr. Clements . . . I must speak with you, sir."

He stiffened and scowled. "Don't make trouble for me. I don't know who you are."

"You have nothing to fear from me, sir."

"Don't be impertinent!" He pushed past her, but she caught at his sleeve.

"Wait! . . . Please! . . . I'm Kayla O'Brian! You must remember!"

He brushed her hand aside and strode away toward the music room.

She started after him, then stopped. It would do no good to confront him before the others. For some reason he was afraid to speak to her, afraid to admit he knew her. She sank into a chair in the morning room even though she wasn't supposed to. "I will not give up so easily," she whispered. "Thank You, Heavenly Father, for Your help and Your strength. Soften the heart of Mr. Clements so he will speak with me and help me."

Just then Priscilla slipped into the morning room and closed the door behind her. Her face was white, and tears stood in her wide blue eyes. "At last! Where have you been, Megan? I need you."

Kayla rushed to her side, led her to the sofa, and sat beside her. "What is it, Mrs. Tweed?"

"Mrs. Tweed! Call me Priscilla or I'll go mad!" She tugged at her lace handkerchief as she faced Kayla. "Mrs. Loftus started talking politics to me. She has met President Cleveland, and she seemed to think I was a nobody because I haven't." Priscilla lowered her voice. "To tell the truth I didn't even remember the President's name. Isn't that terrible? She treated me as if I have half a brain."

"You wipe away those tears and walk right back inside. Talk with Mrs. Loftus about things you do know about. Can she play the piano? Can she sing? You have talents. And you have a brain. If you want to know about politics, then learn about politics. Next time you meet Mrs. Loftus you can talk to her about President Cleveland and even about his Vice president."

Priscilla dabbed away her tears with her handkerchief and nodded. "Thank you, Megan."

"My name is Kayla O'Brian."

"I can walk back inside with my head high."

"That you can!"

"Oh, I don't want to have another party as long as I live!"

"If Mr. Tweed wants one, you can manage it. You can do anything through Christ who gives you strength."

"I can?" Priscilla sniffed and blinked back tears.

Kayla smiled and nodded.

Priscilla lifted her chin. "Yes, I can! You know, Megan, I believe I'll even learn how to pray on my own. And read my Bible. After all, you won't always be around to help me."

"No, I won't. I must get back to my brother."

"Mr. Tweed said you have no family."

"I have Timothy."

"Why don't you bring him here? He can work for us too. What can he do?"

Kayla shook her head. "No . . . Timothy and I are going to Maryland to train horses on Briarwood Farms."

Priscilla's face clouded over. "But you can't do that. You must stay with us for three and a half years . . . Mr. Tweed said so."

"He was wrong."

"That can't be."

"But it is."

Priscilla jumped up with a chipper laugh. "I'm all right now. I'll go back to my guests. And I'll talk about music to Mrs. Loftus." She ran lightly to the door, then turned. "Thanks, Megan. You better get out of here before Mr. Tweed scolds you for sitting down on the job."

With a sigh Kayla followed Priscilla out of the room.

8

Kayla stood at the open door to usher the guests out as their carriages or buggies were driven up. Covered lamps lit the way from the door to the carriage step. The air had turned cooler, but Kayla liked the brisk feel of the wind. A dog barked somewhere behind the house. Laughter floated across the wide lawn. Mr. and Mrs. Clements stepped out, and Kayla's heart sank. She hadn't been able to speak alone with Mr. Clements. He'd walked away each time she'd gotten close to him. She looked longingly at him, but he wouldn't glance in her direction. Just as he started toward his buggy he dropped his hat. She bent to pick it up for him just as he did. Their hands touched at the hat, and he pushed a folded paper into her palm. She lifted a brow questioningly, but he shook his head slightly. Her heart hammered, and she was sure the others could hear it. She kept the folded paper hidden in her palm, anxious to get alone and read it. It burned her skin as she sent each guest to his or her buggy.

Had Amee seen the exchange between herself and Mr. Clements? Several times she shot a warning look at Kayla, but Kayla only smiled.

While the Tweeds said a long good-bye to their last guests Amee whispered, "What's wrong with you, Megan? You're acting strange . . . And Mr. Tweed noticed."

Kayla sucked in her breath. She dare not do anything to make Mr. Tweed suspicious. "I am tired, Amee." That she was, but also excited and anxious to see what Mr. Clements had pressed into her hand.

Later, after Amee had already gone upstairs, Kayla walked across the wide hall. She wanted to run to the nearest lamp and see what she held in her hand, but the Tweeds were behind her.

"Megan . . ." called Mr. Tweed.

She turned slowly at the tone of his voice. "Sir?" She was glad for the semi-darkness which kept him from being able to see the flush that spread over her neck and face.

He took a step toward her. "Must I lock you in your room tonight?"

Kayla gasped. "Oh, that would be terrible!"

Priscilla touched her husband's hand. "Warton, Megan is tired and wants to go to bed. So do I."

His face softened as he looked down at his wife. "Then we'll go right up." He slipped an arm around her narrow waist and pulled her to his side.

Kayla watched them walk to the grand stairway that was still well-lit.

Mr. Tweed glanced over his shoulder at her. "You may go to bed, Megan. I'll speak with you in the morning."

She hoped to be gone before he had the chance, so she didn't nod. "Good night, Mr. Tweed . . . Mrs. Tweed."

Priscilla smiled back at Megan and mouthed, "Thank you."

Kayla nodded. "Thank you," she whispered. She was glad that someone else would turn out the lamps and snuff out the candles. If she had to wait much longer to see the paper in her hand she would burst.

In the kitchen she picked up the small lamp she was to carry to her room. The wick was low, but she could see as she walked up the narrow back stairs. Suddenly she stopped. She could not wait another minute. She had to see what Andrew Clements had given her.

She sank onto a step and set the lamp on the ledge above. Shadows danced on the wall. Slowly she opened her hand to see what she held. Was the folded piece of paper a note of warning or of help?

Her heart thudded and seemed to echo in the stairwell. The paper crackled as she opened it. *Kayla O'Brian* was written in fancy script at the top. "He knows me," she whispered, but she really wanted to shout it from the rooftops. *I want to help you for what you did for me, but I dare not admit that I saw you in the alley. I will pick you up at midnight and take you away. A.C.*

She held it closer to the light and read it again, then again. Shivers ran up and down her spine. "Midnight," she whispered, smiling. Oh, but it had to be almost midnight already. She had to change into her own clothes and shoes.

Upstairs she set the lamp on the lampstand and looked around the tiny room that held a small bed, chest of drawers, and four hooks with clothes on them. Frantically she searched for her dress, but it was gone. What had Amee done with it? Was it still in the room where she'd taken her bath?

She picked up the lamp and tiptoed down the hall to the room. The tub was empty. A chamber pot stood to the side of it. Towels hung on a wooden rod on the wall. Her dress wasn't there either. Slowly she walked back down the hall. Snores as loud as Sean Murphy's poured from under the door of a room beside Amee's and filled the hallway.

Suddenly Amee's door opened. She stood in her nightgown and cap with her lamp held high. Her feet were bare, and her hair hung down her shoulders in two long braids. "Why are you creeping around, Megan?" she whispered sharply.

"I was looking for my dress and shoes."

"Your things are in your room."

"Those aren't mine. I only have what I wore here today."

"I gave them to Juniper to wash and use for rags. The shoes I told Juniper she could keep."

"No!"

"Shhh! Do you want to wake the others?" Amee stepped close to Kayla. "You have clothes in your room that are new and clean. Don't fret about the rags you had on before."

Kayla sighed and nodded. They were indeed only clothes even though they had been Mama's. The important thing was to get away to meet Mr. Clements at midnight. She managed a smile. "Good night, Amee. Sleep well."

"You too, Megan. And don't make me call you Kayla. I'm too tired." She walked into her room and gently closed the door.

In her room Kayla pulled off the uniform and slipped on a cotton street dress that brushed the floor. She buttoned all the tiny buttons and tied the belt at the back of her waist. The only other pair of shoes looked serviceable and comfortable. She pulled them on to find they fit much better than the ones she'd worn all evening. Her hands shaking, she tucked the note in her sleeve and buttoned her cuff. She walked to the door, stopped, and looked back. Was she daft to walk away from a clean room and plenty of food, plus a wage each week?

"I must leave. 'Tis no question about it!"

She thought of Amee's kindness and Priscilla's need. "I can't just walk out without a word to them," she muttered.

On the chest she found a box of paper and a pencil. She wrote:

Dear Amee,

Thank you for your help. I am glad I got to meet you. I must go to Timothy. You are a nice girl. Do remember that Jesus does love you and miracles really do happen.

I am yours truly,
Kayla O'Brian

Kayla folded the note, wrote Amee's name on the outside of it, and laid it on the pillow on the bed where Amee would be sure to see it in the morning. If Amee couldn't read, she could find someone who would read it to her. On another paper Kayla wrote:

Dear Priscilla Tweed,

You have a kind heart. Remember always that God is your strength through Christ. Do read the Bible and pray every day. Tell Mr. Tweed that I am indeed
Kayla O'Brian

With a heavy sigh Kayla folded the note, wrote Priscilla's name on it, and dropped it beside Amee's note. "Heavenly Father, thank You for taking care of these two."

Now she could leave.

A few minutes later she stood in the dark kitchen. She smelled coffee and the sourdough rising at the back of the range. A clock from another room bonged twelve. Her stomach fluttered. She found the skeleton key still in the lock, unlocked the door, and slipped outside. Cool wind blew against her flushed skin. A night bird called. From far away a bell rang.

Would Mr. Clements keep his word and meet her?

What if Mr. Tweed found her outside the house? She shivered. It was too terrible to think about.

Her skirts held high away from the dew-wet grass, she crept around to the street and waited at the base of a huge maple. In the distance she heard the steady pounding of hoofbeats. It was a lone rider. He stopped. She couldn't tell if it was Mr. Clements, but she did recognize the big roan. Carefully she stepped away from the tree.

"Kayla O'Brian?" said the man.

"Mr. Clements?"

"Yes . . . Hurry!"

She ran lightly to the big roan, and Mr. Clements lifted her easily to sit behind him. The roan leaped ahead, his hoofbeats suddenly too loud for Kayla. Surely the sound would send Mr. Tweed to his window and he'd see her fleeing.

Mr. Clements said over his shoulder, "We must get away before Tweed sees us."

"Why didn't you tell him who I was?"

"I'll explain later."

She trembled. Dare she trust him? What if he was taking her into more danger than she'd been in yet?

"Where do you want to go?" he asked.

She hadn't thought that far ahead. "I must find my brother." She felt as if she was shouting.

"Where is he?"

"I don't know. I last saw him at the docks . . . We were staying with Sean Murphy."

He reined the roan to a walk, and she told him where

Sean Murphy lived, but she also told him about Hope Murphy signing them over to the Children's Aid Society.

"I could take you to the Society."

"No! They want to take us west." She told him about the work on Briarwood Farms. "Timothy and I will go to Maryland just as we planned."

He nodded. "Just so you get out of the city before you're forced to live off the streets. I'll take you to the Murphys and see if Timothy is with them."

Kayla agreed. She was quiet a while. "Mr. Clements?"

"What?"

"Why wouldn't you tell Mr. Tweed who I really am?"

"I couldn't take the chance. It's a long and complicated story. This is not the time to explain."

"I left Amee and Mrs. Tweed good-bye notes."

"You what?" he cried.

She trembled at his anger. "I could not go away without a word and have them worry."

"Where did you leave the notes?"

"On the pillow in the bedroom they put me in . . . In the attic."

"So, probably no one will find the notes until morning." He blew out his breath and tugged his hat lower on his forehead. "It doesn't give me much time."

"To do what?"

"There's not time to go into it."

"I'm sorry if I made things hard for you."

"You didn't know." He urged the roan into a trot.

Kayla didn't speak again except to give Mr. Clements directions to Sean Murphy's. Wind whipped against her, fluttering her skirts. Pins flew from her hair, and her long braid

75

flipped down her back. Soon she'd find Timothy! Excitement bubbled inside her.

"Timothy," she mouthed.

She would find him, wouldn't she? Oh, she had to!

Mr. Clements stopped his roan outside the Murphys' room. Kayla leaped to the bricks and ran to the door, Mr. Clements behind her. He reached around her and rapped sharply. The sound was loud. Kayla pressed her hand to her racing heart. Finally Sean Murphy opened the door, a lamp in his hand. He looked tired and still half-asleep.

"What do you want?" he asked.

"Is Timothy here?" asked Kayla, trying to peek past Sean into the cluttered room.

He bent down and peered into her face. "Kayla! Timothy said somebody dragged you off!"

"Someone did," said Mr. Clements. "I brought her back to get her brother . . . Then they're going with me."

Sean's brows shot up. "I'll have none of that! They're staying right here!"

"Is Timothy here?" asked Kayla in a strangled voice.

"Of course."

Mr. Clements pushed his hat to the back of his head. "I won't let the girl stay here only to have your wife make more trouble for her."

"I resent that!"

"Resent it all you like. Call the boy out here. They're going with me."

Sean finally turned, but Timothy was already there. He ducked under Sean's arm and flung himself against Kayla. She hugged him hard. She smelled his dirty hair and body, but right now even that didn't matter.

"It does my heart good to see you, Timothy!"

"I was afraid you were dead or something," he said, sounding close to tears.

She patted his arm. "Get our things, Timothy. We're going with this man."

"I can't let you go," said Sean. "I vowed to your papa that I'd watch out for you."

"I release you from your vow, Sean Murphy," said Kayla.

Timothy brought the two cases they'd carried to the docks that morning. "That's all we have. *She* sold the rest today while we were gone."

"I'm sorry for what Hope did," said Sean, obviously embarrassed. "You must excuse her. She's got it hard with such a family and not enough food for them."

"Good-bye, Sean Murphy," said Kayla and Timothy in one voice.

"Good-bye," said Sean gruffly. "I did my best for you two."

Kayla took a case from Timothy, and they walked down the brick street—away from Sean Murphy and away from Hope Murphy and hopefully away from the filth and the hunger. Mr. Clements led the big roan and walked beside them. Kayla told Timothy about her adventure, and he told her how he'd run to Sean for help. They'd gone to the police, but they said that without knowing something about Kayla's captor it would be hard to find her.

"I'm happy, I am, that you're safe," said Timothy with a grin.

At the livery Mr. Clements woke the livery man, hired a buggy, tied the roan to the back, and loaded them in. "I'm taking you to a small house several blocks away. You can stay there for the night . . . Then tomorrow we'll see about getting you on the boat to Baltimore."

"Thank you," said Kayla.

"Why are you doing this for us?" asked Timothy suspiciously.

"He's a kind man," said Kayla.

"Because you helped me the other day," said Mr. Clements. "And you didn't rob me."

"We are O'Brians and we don't steal," said Timothy.

Mr. Clements stopped the buggy outside a small house with a tiny yard and flower garden. "Before we go in I must tell you about another guest I have." Mr. Clements cleared his throat. "This house belongs to the woman who was the nanny to my children. She takes in boarders when I need her to."

Kayla looked expectantly at Mr. Clements.

"Inside with Peg is Megan, Tweed's runaway bond servant."

Kayla gasped.

"What's all this about?" asked Timothy sharply.

"Why is she here?" asked Kayla.

"I'll explain later. But let me get you settled inside first." He knocked on the door, and soon it was opened by a woman holding a lamp who looked as if she could be anyone's grandmother. "Hello, Peg. More company for you tonight."

"Come right in, Mr. Clements. Always room for more."

"This is Kayla and her brother Timothy. They need a place for a day or two. Children, this is Granny Peg. If you're hungry she'll find you something to eat." He kissed the top of Peg's white hair. "I could use a thick slice of your apple pie and a cup of black coffee if you have it."

"Surely do." Peg led the way to the small kitchen and sat them at her round table. She poured milk for Kayla and Timothy, coffee for Mr. Clements, then served them all big pieces of apple pie. "I know you want to talk in privacy, so I'll be off to bed again. You show the children where they're to sleep."

He nodded and kissed Peg again. She walked to her room and closed her door.

Timothy dug into his pie, too hungry to wait another minute.

Kayla thankfully took a drink of her milk, dabbed her mouth with a white napkin, then took a bite of pie. She'd never tasted such apple pie since she'd left Ireland.

"I'll explain what's been going on," said Mr. Clements after he'd eaten most of his pie. "I went into a business deal with Tweed and Loftus." He leaned back and quickly explained to Timothy who the men were. "Loftus owns cargo ships. Tweed and I put up money to load the ship with cargo in England to sell here in America. Loftus has since told us the ship went down and we lost everything. But I learned Megan was on the ship that supposedly went down. She said she heard Loftus say that he'd had the ship refitted and reregistered; the ship didn't go down at all. He changed the name and the look of it so that no one would know. I have been investigating the whole thing, and the day I almost ran over you two Loftus and Tweed thought I was out of town. Kayla, I didn't want you to say anything that would endanger my investigation."

"That I can understand, sir."

"I don't know if Tweed is a party to all of this or if he's as innocent as I am. Megan didn't know either. She just knew that she was in real danger, so she ran. Once Tweed caught her and took her back, but the second time he caught you instead."

Kayla locked her hands in her lap. "Do we look that much alike?"

"You do look very much alike. Standing side by side anyone could tell you apart, I'm sure, but apart you look much the same. I saw Loftus watching you at the party, and I could tell he was nervous with you around, so he also must have thought you were Megan."

A shiver ran down Kayla's spine. She was thankful she hadn't known about Mr. Loftus.

"'Tis all Hope Murphy's fault," snapped Timothy.

"Much is," said Kayla grimly.

Mr. Clements sipped his coffee. "Because I don't know if I can trust Tweed, I'm keeping Megan here until this is settled. Since you left the notes at Tweed's house I'll have to hurry things up. I don't want them suspicious about me or they'll run, and I can't yet prove anything. My detectives should have the proof they need in the morning, and we can then have Loftus arrested—and Tweed too if he's guilty." Mr. Clements drained his cup and set it down with a thump. "Tomorrow when this business is settled I'll help you both get on your way to Baltimore."

"Thank you," said Kayla. It would be wonderful finally to be on the ship to Baltimore, then on to Briarwood Farms.

Suddenly someone pounded on the back door. Kayla jumped. Timothy leaped up, almost upsetting his chair, and stood at Kayla's side to protect her. Mr. Clements peeked out the window, then opened the door.

"What is it, Chester?"

Chester held his cap in his hands. He was short with a

81

wrinkled face and matted salt-and-pepper hair. "Things 'er happenin' at the dock that you want to witness. Sidney came to the house to tell you, and I said you were probably here. So he sent me on the run to get you."

"Tell me everything Sidney said."

Chester screwed up his face and worried his cap until it was twisted out of shape. "Somethin' about a girl. They took the girl from Tweed's and on to Loftus at the docks, and he yelled that it was the wrong girl, but now they'd have to get rid of her. He said they'd take her and sell her."

Kayla shivered. Could they have kidnapped Amee?

"They said they was going after the right girl. Thompson rode to Tweed's to keep them from going inside again."

Mr. Clements grabbed his hat. "I'll get right to the docks."

"Let me go too!" cried Kayla, catching his arm. "I want to help."

"No!" Timothy jerked Kayla away from Mr. Clements. "You'll get hurt."

Mr. Clements looked thoughtfully at Kayla. "I have a plan . . . and I do need your help." He turned to Timothy. "I'll take good care of her. You can come if you want, as long as you stay out of sight."

Kayla shivered as Mr. Clements quickly outlined his plan to them.

"Chester, get right back to Sidney and tell him what we're going to do. We're going to get Bracken Loftus *tonight*. And Tweed if he's guilty."

Several minutes later Kayla walked quietly beside Mr. Clements to *The Sea Mate*. Her hair was in tangles around her head, and he had a tight grip on her arm.

"Hello, *Sea Mate*. Bracken Loftus, I have a prize for you," called Mr. Clements. He whispered to Kayla, "Scream. Make it good."

She tipped back her head and screamed until her throat hurt.

"Quiet!" shouted Mr. Clements, clamping a hand over her mouth.

She sagged against him just as he'd told her to, then struggled as if she were trying to get away. She hoped Timothy would remember that she was only pretending and not leap out of his hiding-place to save her.

Just then Bracken Loftus walked down the gangplank. "Clements . . . What brings you here?"

"Megan . . . She told me a wild tale. At first I didn't believe her, but now I do."

Loftus stopped a foot from Mr. Clements and Kayla. He scowled at Kayla. "So why did you bring her here?"

"I didn't want her going to the authorities with her story."

Loftus moved restlessly. "What do you think I want with her?"

Mr. Clements laughed. "I know you don't want her to report what she knows."

Kayla struggled again, and Mr. Clements snapped at her to be quiet.

Loftus pulled off his hat and rubbed his head. "What's in this for you, Clements?"

"My money back . . . with interest."

"And I get the girl."

"Of course. Sell her where no one can speak English or understand what she tells them." Mr. Clements pushed Kayla toward Loftus, then jerked her back. "Before I hand her over, I want my money."

"You'll get it."

"What about Tweed?"

"Tweed knows nothing of this."

"He doesn't know that you refitted and reregistered your ship?"

"No . . . And I don't want him knowing. If you tell him I'll call you a liar. It'll be your word against mine."

"We've heard enough," said Clements. "Sidney!"

Suddenly the dock was full of men. One grabbed Loftus, while others swarmed onto the ship. Timothy ran to Kayla's side, and they huddled together, watching the action. Soon one of the men brought Amee out, sobbing hysterically.

Kayla reached out for her and held her close. "You're safe now, Amee. You can go to Tweed's and sleep safely and peacefully."

"Megan, how did you get here?"

"She's Kayla O'Brian," snapped Timothy. "And I'm her brother Timothy."

Amee wiped the back of her hand across her nose as she looked from Timothy to Kayla. "You really are Kayla O'Brian?"

"That I am!"

"Megan is safe," said Mr. Clements. "She knew what Loftus did, and he wanted her silenced. Now that I know Mr. Tweed wasn't in on any of this, I'll see that Megan is returned."

Amee giggled nervously. "You just never know what's going on. I never really believed you, Kayla. I'm sorry." She pushed a strand of hair out of her face "What will you do now, Kayla?"

"Timothy and I are going to Maryland." She hugged Amee. "I left a note for you and for Priscilla Tweed."

"I can't read."

"Ask Priscilla to read it to you. She needs a friend."

"But I'm only a servant."

"You can be both." Kayla hugged her again, then watched her walk away with two men who were taking her safely home.

Mr. Clements slipped an arm around Kayla and clamped a hand on Timothy's shoulder. "I'll get you children to Granny Peg so you can get some sleep before daylight comes."

Kayla yawned. In the excitement she'd forgotten that she was tired. Tomorrow she and Timothy would make their final plans to go to Maryland. But first she'd see that Timothy had a bath and a haircut.

Nothing would stop them this time.

10

Kayla stood back from Timothy and smiled. Granny Peg had given them the run of the house while she rode to the Tweeds with Megan. "Timothy, you smell nice and clean, and your hair looks as it should."

He touched his head and wrinkled his nose. "Am I bald?"

"No, but it is a short cut so that it will stay well-trimmed all the way to Maryland."

He rubbed his head and chuckled. "Briarwood Farms! 'Tis a happy day for sure." The smiled vanished, and he scowled. "But it will be a long while before I can forgive what Hope Murphy did to us."

"I know." Kayla sat down and leaned her elbows on the table. "We will need to remember what Papa always said."

"What is that?"

"'The Devil himself works through people to hurt God's children.' Papa said to be angry at the Devil, not at the person hurting us."

Timothy's face hardened as he leaned forward in his chair. "Hope Murphy deserves our anger."

Kayla sighed. "That she does."

"I tried to make her give me the money she got from sell-ing our stuff, but she'd already spent it on food. Sean Murphy said he would pay us back once he had the money. But I know that won't happen. Not with six babes to feed and clothe."

Kayla twisted the end of her braid around her finger. "We will still make something good come out of what Satan meant for harm." She told him how she'd been able to survive at the Tweeds by doing things for others and by working as if she was working for Jesus Himself. "God has a purpose for our lives, Timothy, and well you know it. Wherever we are, we will be like Jesus — caring, loving, and kind."

Timothy groaned. "I cannot be like that!"

"With God's help you can, Timothy."

Finally he nodded. "With God's help."

Kayla swept up the black hair on the floor and threw it away, then opened her case. She lifted out the bag. "At least we still have the letter from Briarwood Farms."

"That we do." Timothy leaned over the bag with her.

She reached into the bag and searched through the diary and the Bible. Her heart thundered in her ears. Slowly she turned to Timothy. "'Tis gone," she whispered barely loud enough for him to hear.

Timothy threw back his head and howled at the top of his lungs much like a wounded animal would do.

She patted his arm to calm him. "We won't let this destroy us, Timothy. We'll get the letter from Hope Murphy, and we'll get it now."

"I will shake it out of her, babe or no!"

"We must not wait for Mr. Clements. We must go to Hope Murphy this very moment." Kayla pushed the bag into the case and strapped the case closed.

Timothy pounded the table with his fist. "That woman!"

"I'll leave a note with Granny Peg for Mr. Clements." Kayla felt dizzy with anger as she searched for a scrap of paper. Hot tears blurred her vision. Finally she found some paper and quickly wrote to Mr. Clements, thanking him for all he'd done for them. The writing was not her usual fine script, but it had to do.

Cases in hand, they walked outdoors into the pleasant warm September day. Clouds dotted the blue sky. A bird sang in a nearby pine.

"This I cannot forgive," muttered Kayla as she marched along. "'Tis too much to ask."

"I hate her," snapped Timothy.

Kayla stopped short. "You cannot hate her, Timothy O'Brian!"

"I hate her anyway."

Kayla closed her mouth and walked on. Hate burned in her heart too, hate like she'd never felt before. Perspiration dampened her dress, the same dress she'd worn last night. Mr. Clements had told her to keep it since her "captors" had kept her dress. He said he'd pay Mr. Tweed for it, so she'd agreed to keep it and wear it.

It was midmorning by the time they reached the tenement building and Hope Murphy's room. Taking a deep breath, Kayla set down her case, then knocked.

Hope Murphy opened the door and gasped at the sight of them. She tried to slam it shut, but Timothy pushed against it and she stumbled back.

"We came for our letter," said Kayla in an icy voice.

Hope dropped to a chair, and the babes clung to her legs. The boys were outdoors. With a shaking hand she hooked a strand of hair behind her ear. "I sold the letter."

"Sold it!" cried Timothy.

"Sold it?" asked Kayla in shock.

Hope barely nodded. "To a man who wanted the job."

"How could you?" Kayla pressed her fingers to her temples. Would her head burst with the anger she felt?

"It brought me enough so we could move from this place into a small house." Hope flicked away her tears. "I could not raise my babes in this place! The people at Briarwood Farms wouldn't really take two children in place of Patrick O'Brian."

Kayla leaned down with her face almost touching Hope's. "Where is the man? Tell us and we'll get the letter back!" She clutched her own dress so she wouldn't grab Mrs. Murphy and shake her like a dog shakes a stick. "Where is he?"

Hope swallowed hard. "Let me think."

"Where is he?" asked Timothy, his fists doubled at his sides. He wanted to hit her, but that he could not do.

Mary and Angel burst into tears. Hope picked up Mary and rubbed Angel's head. "You're scaring the children."

"Where is the man?" asked Kayla in a low, tight voice.

Suddenly Hope brightened. "I remember . . . He said he was leaving today on a paddleboat called *Columbus* . . . from the South Street Seaport."

"Give us the money and we'll take it to him," said Timothy.

"But I don't have the money. I used it to secure the house. But if you bring him back with the letter, I'll get the money back from the house." Hope sighed. "Even though it will break my babe's hearts."

"What is the man's name?" asked Timothy.

Hope bit her lip. "Stone . . . Wyatt Stone."

"What does he look like?" asked Kayla.

"Short and slight with brown hair and dark eyes. About my age. And he wears a beaver top hat like the Bowery Boys."

Kayla strode to the door, then turned. "We'll be back."

"That we will!" Timothy closed the door behind them, and they picked up their cases and walked toward the South Street Seaport. They'd both been there before.

Several minutes later they reached their destination. "Timothy, stay close now. We don't want to get separated in this mob." Kayla had to shout to be heard.

He nodded.

Kayla wanted to hold her nose against the dead-fish smell. Her ears rang with the many sounds. Finally she spotted the *Columbus*, and she pointed the paddleboat out to Timothy.

They marched right up the gangplank along with many others, and when the captain stopped them Kayla said, "We're here to see Wyatt Stone."

The captain wrinkled his round face in thought. "Stone . . . Ah, yes . . . He's below in the steerage." He told them how to get below, then turned to two men.

Kayla hadn't expected it would be so easy. She walked across the deck with Timothy beside her and went below, only to find as great a crowd there as on deck. They set their cases beside other baggage to make it easier to walk through the crowd. After a long time Kayla spotted the man she was sure must be Wyatt Stone. He was surrounded with ragged children. Kayla's heart lightened. If the man liked children enough to take time for them, he would surely give them back their letter.

She pushed as close to him as she could get, but still wasn't close enough to speak to him in a normal voice. "Mr. Stone," she called, standing on tiptoe.

He lifted his head and frowned. "Wait your turn."

Kayla sighed and waited while Mr. Stone flipped through a notebook, stopping on occasion to write something down. "What is he doing?" she asked Timothy.

"I can't see," said Timothy, jumping high, but still unable to see.

Finally the crowd moved enough that she stood beside Wyatt Stone. "I'm Kayla O'Brian," she said.

"And I'm Timothy O'Brian," he said. "We came to talk to you."

"Wait!" He held up a hand, then flipped through his book. "Ah ha! I found you. You're in order, so you may wait over there." He motioned toward the baggage area. "Go, go, go." He waved his hand as if he was brushing them away. "Go."

"But we must speak to you," said Kayla.

"Later . . . Please . . . I have to finish here first. But I will get to you, I promise. We have a lot to talk about."

"About Briarwood Farms," said Timothy.

"Yes," he said. "Go! Wait over there . . . Please."

Kayla sighed and pushed her way back to wait where he'd said. She sat on her case, with Timothy beside her on his. "He seems nice," she said.

"That he does. But I have this strange feeling that all's not well." Timothy rubbed his hand over his worn pants leg.

"Oh, but it smells in here! Look at all those children. They look dirty. And they're so noisy." Kayla watched them for several minutes. A girl about five was crying all alone, and Kayla wanted to comfort her, but she stayed where Mr. Stone had said to wait.

"Here comes, Mr. Stone." Timothy jumped up with Kayla beside him.

Mr. Stone pushed his way through the crowd, but it seemed as if the crowd was following him.

"Mr. Stone . . ." called Kayla.

He smiled at her and waved. "Follow me," he shouted.

Kayla and Timothy joined the crowd and walked back

up on deck. People lined the rail. Some shouted and waved to people on the wharf. Some of the children pushed their way to the rail and looked over it, talking and laughing. Some were crying. One girl yelled, "I want to stay! Don't make me go!"

"Gangplank's coming up!" shouted a boy.

Kayla frowned. Did he mean the gangplank to this boat? She couldn't see. Mr. Stone would tell them if the boat had cast off, wouldn't he?

She watched him once again push his way toward them. He looked tired but cheerful.

"Now, what can I do for you two? O'Brian, correct?"

"Yes. I'm Kayla and my brother is Timothy."

"I'm pleased you're here." He shook hands with Timothy and smiled at Kayla. "This is a big step for you."

"They're casting off!" shouted a boy near them. "We're on our way!" He grabbed the boy beside him and playfully wrestled him to the deck.

Kayla frowned. Did the boys mean the boat was leaving? She glanced at Timothy, but he didn't seem to be concerned, so she shrugged it off.

"This is quite an adventure," said Mr. Stone.

"Mr. Stone, we came about the letter," said Kayla.

He lifted a fine brow. "Yes?"

"Hope Murphy sent us," said Timothy.

"Yes . . . Mrs. Murphy. And how is she today?"

Timothy wanted to say just what he thought of Mrs. Murphy, but he let Kayla do the talking.

"She's fine." Kayla suddenly lost her balance and bumped against Mr. Stone. She blushed and pulled back. "I'm sorry, sir."

"You'll get your sea legs before long," he said with a

93

chuckle. "Some get them immediately and others after a while, but there are some who never do."

"The letter, Mr. Stone," said Kayla.

Just then several boys ran past, shouting in anger.

"Boys!" snapped Mr. Stone. "Don't run!"

They looked back at him, then kept right on running.

"I must see to them," he said. "I'll talk to you later."

Timothy blocked his way. "We want the letter Mrs. Murphy sold you. She'll give back your money."

Mr. Stone pushed his hat to the back of his head as he studied Timothy. "I don't believe I know what you're talking about."

Kayla pitched forward, but this time caught her balance before she fell against Mr. Stone. A loud clacking of paddle wheels and the noisy splash of water almost covered all the other sounds. Suddenly Kayla realized the boat was indeed moving away from shore. She gripped Mr. Stone's arm. "Oh, we must get off!"

"Just relax . . . You've nothing to fear," said Mr. Stone, patting her hand.

Timothy stumbled, but caught himself before he fell into the woman walking past. "Are we moving?" he asked in alarm.

Mr. Stone frowned slightly. "Children, I don't know what's going on here. Of course we're moving."

Kayla gasped. "Just who are you?"

"You know who I am. Wyatt Stone . . . Children's Aid Society."

Kayla cried out, "Where are we going?"

"To Albany, of course," said Mr. Stone.

Timothy pushed his way to the rail and watched the docks and the jumble of buildings grow smaller and smaller. He scrambled up on the rail, ready to jump overboard, but Mr. Stone hauled him back.

"Do you want to kill yourself? Don't try that again, young man!"

Kayla burst into tears and wept aloud.

"Don't be frightened," said Mr. Stone.

She sobbed harder. For once she didn't care that she was making a spectacle of herself. Their lives were ruined. They had no letter, and they had no future on Briarwood Farms. They were going west even if they didn't want to go.

Timothy put his arms around her and pushed his face against her shoulder. He wanted to cry, but anger held back his tears. He held Kayla without speaking, his eyes squeezed tightly shut.

Scalding tears streamed down Kayla's cheeks, and sobs tore from her throat.

11

Kayla wrapped her arms around herself and rocked back and forth while the paddle wheels turned and people walked the deck in the cool evening air. Her throat ached from crying so hard. She still felt tears inside, but they seemed locked in place. Timothy had gone to find them something to eat, but she didn't want to eat—not now, not ever.

Mr. Stone bent down to Kayla. She looked at him, then closed her eyes. "Kayla, I want you to meet Ruth Harrison. She's with the Children's Aid Society, and she's here to help with the girls going west."

Kayla peeked at Ruth Harrison as she knelt beside her. She looked to be just a little older than Priscilla Tweed. But unlike Priscilla, Ruth Harrison was a plain, tiny woman with an ugly white scar on the left side of her face. "Will you let me help you?" Her voice was low and pleasant.

Kayla glanced at the woman, then quickly away. "No."

"It hurts me to see you so upset."

Kayla rocked harder.

"I'll take you below where you can lie down." Ruth tried

97

to lift Kayla, but she shook her off. "You can't sit out here all night."

Kayla trembled, stopped rocking, and looked into Ruth's face. "We . . . want . . . to go to . . . Maryland."

Ruth patted Kayla's back. "I'm so sorry. Mr. Stone told me what happened. If we could take you to Baltimore, we would. But we can't."

"Just let us leave!"

"But we can't do that either. We're in charge of you now until we find you a nice family."

Kayla shook her head and moaned. "We don't need a family."

"But you do. And there are people who are waiting to adopt you. There are people who need you as much as you need them."

"We came from County Offaly just to work at Briarwood Farms."

"But your parents died, and you can't go there on your own."

Kayla fell back as if she'd been struck. It hurt too much to hear someone say her parents were dead. She knew they were, but she didn't let herself think about it. She had refused to watch when they were buried at sea. And if she pretended hard enough she could see them already at Briarwood Farms waiting for her and Timothy to get there.

Ruth sat beside Kayla and took her hand. "Tell me about your mama and papa. What were their names?"

Kayla bit her trembling lip and looked as if she would burst into tears again. Finally she said, "Patrick and Megan O'Brian."

"Nice Irish names."

Kayla rubbed her thumbnail. "Papa was the best horse trainer in all of Ireland."

"Was he?"

"It didn't matter how wild the horse, Papa could train it to obey every command. He had the best jumpers and the best trotters. But what he liked best was training thoroughbreds for racing." In her mind's eye Kayla could see Papa working with his horses in the special arena he'd built. Oh, she was so proud of him! "He taught Timothy and me everything he knew about horses."

"What about your mama?"

Kayla twisted her braid around her finger and looked off across the calm water. "Mama . . . Mama loved us all so much! She could tell a fine story and make you laugh or make you cry. Nobody could bake a pie like Mama. Her flower garden and her vegetable garden were grand to behold." Kayla touched her cheek, her hair, her dark brows. "I look like Mama . . . Same black hair and blue eyes. I did grow a little taller. When we left Ireland I was short, and while we traveled I grew so much I grew out of all my clothes so that I had to wear Mama's. I have her clothes and her shoes . . ." Kayla took a deep breath. "Her Bible . . . Her diary." Kayla's voice broke. "But Hope Murphy sold her good china dishes and all her other things."

"Have you read her diary?"

"No. I touched it once, but I cannot read it." Fresh tears filled Kayla's eyes.

"Did your mama and papa love Jesus?"

"Yes."

"So they are in Heaven. Instead of moving to Briarwood Farms, they moved to Heaven. Someday you'll see them there."

"But I want them now!"

"I know." Ruth rubbed Kayla's arm. "I know."

Kayla sat quietly for a long time. She didn't notice when Timothy sat beside her, or when Ruth left her to tend to the other children. She watched the sky darken and the stars come out. Over the splash of water on the paddle wheels she heard the loud music and laughter from the saloon above deck. Timothy fell asleep beside her. Finally she noticed him there, and she touched him gently, softly. She still had her Timothy. She saw the crackers and apple he'd brought to her, and she felt the first stirrings of hunger. Slowly she ate the crisp apple together with the crackers. She moved her cramped muscles until she was comfortable.

"Timothy," she whispered, "we will not be going to Briarwood Farms. We are going west. We must accept that." Her voice broke. Could he accept that? Could she?

Mama and Papa were not waiting for them at Briarwood Farms like she wished they were. But they were in Heaven!

Suddenly Kayla remembered something Mama had said: "Kayla, when I get to Heaven, after I see Jesus and after I worship God for a while I'm going to find Miriam and have her teach me the dance of victory that she danced."

A picture of Mama doing a victory dance flashed in Kayla's mind, and she smiled. "Oh, Mama."

Timothy stirred. "Kayla?"

"I'm here."

He sat up beside her and leaned against her. "Are you all right?"

"I don't know."

"We won't be going to Briarwood Farms," he said.

100

She sighed heavily. "That I know."

"Mr. Stone says there are lots of farms west. Would you be happy on a farm somewhere besides Maryland?"

She turned to look into his eyes. "Will you?"

"I will try," whispered Timothy with a catch in his voice.

"I will try too," said Kayla. She settled back, and he again leaned against her, just as they both used to lean against Mama and Papa.

"One of the boys said we might get adopted by different families."

"That I will not let happen!" Kayla's voice rang out with conviction. "I give you my word."

He sighed. "Hope Murphy is a wicked, wicked woman."

"That she is."

"I shall hate her forever."

Kayla nodded. "As shall I." She felt a tinge of guilt, but brushed it aside. Hope Murphy had brought them pain and agony and the loss of a dream. Kayla pressed her lips tightly together. Hope Murphy deserved to be hated.

Several minutes later Ruth walked back to Kayla. "Shall we go below to sleep? We wouldn't want someone walking on you two during the night, would we?"

Slowly Kayla stood with Timothy beside her. "Timothy, let's be going to bed."

He yawned and walked below with her. The smell smote her, and she wanted to turn back. She looked around at all the sleeping children on mats around the room — boys on one side, girls another. Several snored. One ground his teeth. Two girls sobbed in their sleep. Ruth settled Timothy down near Mr. Stone, who himself was fast asleep and softly snoring, then walked Kayla across to an empty mat.

Kayla stretched out on the mat, and Ruth spread a light blanket over her.

"Sleep well," whispered Ruth. She touched Kayla's brow. "Our Father in Heaven, thank You for loving Kayla. May she sleep in peace this night. In Jesus' name, Amen."

Kayla closed her eyes, and the swaying of the boat rocked her to sleep almost immediately.

12

Kayla stood on the outskirts of the crowd of ragged orphans and looked around the railroad yard. She felt lonely and frightened. Ruth Harrison, Wyatt Stone, and Tom Drake struggled to keep the children off the tracks and away from other passengers. Too many of the children knew the fine art of picking pockets, and even though they'd promised they'd left it behind them, Kayla knew from hearing them talk that they couldn't be trusted. A train whistled, and she jumped. Immigrants talked in languages she couldn't understand, while several boys walked through the crowd hawking sandwiches and apples. Soot fluttered down and landed on her. She brushed at it, only to leave a streak of black instead.

She turned to say something to Timothy, but he wasn't standing beside her. Her heart lurched. Frantically she looked around, shielding her eyes from the morning sun. Finally she spotted him talking to two boys his age, and she sighed in relief. This morning when she'd awakened the thought had crossed her mind that Timothy might try to run away and get to Maryland on his own. When she'd found him still asleep she'd breathed easier.

An immigrant ran through the crowd and knocked down a tiny girl right at Kayla's feet. The man kept running, but the girl burst into tears. Kayla bent to pick her up.

"Don't touch me!" screamed the girl, then swore as badly as the dockworkers and the street boys.

Kayla gripped the girl's thin arms and shook her. "Stop that! You ought not say those terrible words."

The girl frowned. She tugged her ragged dress into place and brushed her dirty blonde hair out of her eyes. "What terrible words?"

"The ones you just said."

The girl knuckled away her tears. "You the crybaby from the boat?"

Kayla flushed as she recalled yesterday's tears. "I'm Kayla O'Brian. What's your name?"

The girl studied Kayla suspiciously and finally answered, "Apple."

"Apple? Is that a nickname?"

"It's my name."

"How old are you, Apple?"

"Four, I think."

"How'd you get your name?"

Apple shrugged and looked too old to be only four. "A man found me in an apple crate when I was one, and he gave me Apple for a name."

"Who raised you?"

"This one and that one, then I raised myself."

"But where is your family?"

"I don't have one." Her dark eyes brightened. "But I'm gonna get one when we get west . . . A mama and daddy and maybe some brothers and sisters. Miss Ruth said so, and she don't lie."

Kayla looked around for Miss Ruth and finally spotted her pulling two fist-fighting girls apart. "Miss Ruth is nice."

"She has an ugly scar. And she won't let nobody tease her about it."

"I wonder how she got it."

Apple folded her arms and tilted her head. "Reggy said he heard her daddy drank too much of the bottle and cut her when he was soused to the gills."

Kayla stared down at Apple. What kind of child was this? "How did you stay alive on your own, Apple?"

She shrugged. "I learned how to take care of myself. But I won't have to no more. Miss Ruth said somebody will be glad to love me and take care of me." Apple smiled dreamily. "I bet my mama will hold me on her lap and sing to me."

"I think you better stop swearing so you don't shock your new family."

"That's what Miss Ruth said, but she didn't tell me what words were good and what ones were bad."

"I'll help you if you want."

Apple stuck out her hand. "Let's shake on it."

Kayla held out her hand and swallowed up Apple's in hers.

Suddenly a stone struck Kayla's leg, and she jumped. "Ouch!" Another one struck her shoulder. "Ouch! Who's doing that?" She shot a look around, but couldn't see who had thrown stones at her. She looked down to speak to Apple, only to find her gone.

Kayla rubbed her leg and shoulder to ease the stinging pain. Why would anyone want to hurt her?

A redheaded girl dressed in a faded dress that reached the calf of her legs stepped up to Kayla. "Hi . . . My name's Clare."

"I'm Kayla O'Brian."

"I'm fourteen."

"So am I."

"You're pretty."

"Thank you."

"See that boy over there? The tall one with blond curls and a blue-and-white striped shirt."

Kayla glanced in the direction Clare pointed. "Yes . . . I see him."

"He thinks you're pretty, but don't get no ideas. Bobby's my beau, and I mean to keep it that way."

Kayla flushed. "I'm not interested in him."

"You think you're too good for him just because you have a last name?"

"No."

"Then why?"

Kayla sighed. "Clare, I don't want any boy as a beau."

"How come?"

"I just don't. When I get older I might . . . if he's like Papa."

Clare wrinkled her nose. "You just remember what I said in case Bobby tries anything with you."

Kayla shuddered as Clare walked back to stand beside Bobby.

Suddenly another stone struck Kayla, this time on the wrist. She jumped and rubbed her wrist. "Who is doing that?" she asked as she looked around. But she couldn't see the guilty person, and no one answered her question. They were all watching immigrants and the conductor talking loudly with wild gestures.

She looked for Timothy, but she couldn't see him. Panic rose in her, and she ran around the mob, jumping up now and then to see over the crowd. Where was Timothy?

Finally she spotted him standing on the track with some boys. She ran to him and grabbed his arm. "Stay with me!"

He pulled away and blushed. "They dared me to stand on the track until the train got to that mark." He pointed a few feet away.

"You will do no such thing!" Kayla jerked him off the track, while the boys teased Timothy about being a sissy.

Timothy stopped short and tried to break free. "Leave me alone, Kayla. You want them all to think I'm some baby?"

"I don't care what they think! I want you alive! I want you beside me all the way west!"

Suddenly a stone struck Kayla on the cheek. "Ouch!" She touched her cheek and touched a trickle of blood.

"Who did that?" yelled Timothy, doubling his fists as he looked all around. "Whoever did that has me to answer to!"

"That should scare 'em," mocked a boy on the track as he laughed and punched the others.

Mr. Drake strode forward, shaking his cane. "Boys, off the track! Get back in the group now!" He turned to Kayla and Timothy. "Don't wander off. Get back with the others."

"Yes, sir," said Timothy.

Kayla lifted her head, and her eyes snapped. How dare Mr. Drake order them about? They weren't unruly and unprincipled like the rest. She wanted to grab Timothy's hand and run back to the wharf and catch the next boat to New York City.

But that was impossible, and she knew it. They had no money, and they had nowhere to go but west.

Slowly, her head down, she walked back to the ragged orphans.

Several minutes later Mr. Drake shouted for the orphans to follow him to the train. Kayla and Timothy picked up their cases where they'd stashed them earlier, then fell into line with the other orphans. Kayla gripped her case even tighter. How she hated being classed as an orphan!

Just then a small boy cut in front of her, stumbled against her, and sent her sprawling to the ground, her skirts flying to her knees. Flushing, she jumped up.

"Are you all right?" asked Timothy in concern.

She nodded.

"That boy bumped against you on purpose," said Timothy. "I tried to grab him, but he was too quick for me."

"Why would he want to knock me down?" Kayla brushed off her skirt and picked up her case again.

"I don't know. To be mean maybe. If I catch him, I'll thrash him good!"

Kayla shook her finger at Timothy. "Don't you be talking like that, Timothy O'Brian. You keep in mind who you are."

He hung his head. "Sometimes 'tis hard to be an O'Brian."

"That it is."

The conductor stopped Mr. Stone before he could board the train. "Full up . . . You and your orphans will have to ride in a boxcar."

"But we have paid-for seats!"

"You got reduced rates, and that means you have seats only if they're available. None are." The conductor's round face was red. He took off his cap and rubbed his thin hair back, then tugged his cap in place. "I'll show you the way. It's a nice enough car, and you'll be comfortable."

Kayla fell into the line that led to the boxcar. None of the orphans spoke, and she knew they felt as frightened as she did. She followed the others up the plank into the car. It was crowded with all of them in there, and she wanted to run back outdoors where there was air and space. There were no windows, and once the door was shut the only light came through the slats. She found a place to set her case, and she sank down with her back against it. Timothy set his case beside hers and dropped to the floor.

The train whistle blew, the car lurched, and they were on their way. Kayla caught Timothy's hand and held it tight.

Kayla felt something crawl across her legs. She leaped up and in the dim light saw a green snake slither toward her case. "A snake!" she screamed.

Several kids scrambled after the snake, turning the boxcar into an uproar.

"How did that get in here?" asked Mr. Stone in agitation.

"Obviously someone brought it during our last stop," said Mr. Drake in an icy voice.

Kayla pushed back her tangled hair. Four days they'd traveled, and each day she'd been frightened or hurt. Miss Ruth said she was sure it was only a coincidence, but Kayla wasn't sure.

"I caught it!" yelled eleven-year-old Martha. Grinning proudly, she held it up as if it was a trophy.

Kayla cringed back.

One of the big boys pushed the door of the boxcar open, letting the sunlight stream in.

"Toss it out," said Mr. Stone.

"I want to keep it," said Martha stubbornly.

"It would die in here," said Miss Ruth. "You wouldn't want that, would you, Martha?"

She thought for a minute, then, holding on to the edge of the door with one hand, carefully tossed the snake into a pile of weeds they were passing.

"Leave the door open," shouted several children, Timothy included. It was exciting to have the door open and watch the passing countryside. Miss Ruth was always frightened that the little ones might fall out.

Kayla breathed deeply to push away the fear as well as to get fresh air. She studied the orphans in the boxcar. Who would bring a snake in? And why put it on her? She shook her head. Maybe it was her imagination.

Mr. Drake called for attention. When everyone was quiet he said, "This next stop is our first stop to leave off some of you. We showed you the map to show you where all we'll stop. There are more than enough families along the way for each of you to find a home." He looked around to make sure he had their attention. "Make yourselves as presentable as possible. Remember your manners. Most of these people are Christians and frown on swearing. Those of you who haven't broken that terrible habit, guard your tongues." He looked right at Apple, and she ducked her head. "When we stop, you all file out and stand in a line. The people will look you over, ask you questions, and then speak to Miss Ruth, Mr. Stone, or myself about you. Feel free to ask them questions too. We want the right children with the right family." He looked around at the solemn faces. "Any questions?"

Reggy lifted his hand.

"Yes, Reggy?"

"I don't want to live on a farm. It's not my style. Can't I find a city family to live with?"

"We'll try, Reggy." Mr. Drake leaned against his cane. "There are a few families from each town who expressed an interest in this 'orphan train,' as many people call it. The towns we'll be stopping at are small, but pleasant, so don't expect another New York City."

Timothy raised his hand.

"Yes, Tim," said Mr. Drake. No matter how often Kayla told him that Timothy was Timothy and not Tim he didn't remember.

"Will you make sure my sister and I go to the same family?"

"Yes . . . We will try our hardest." Mr. Drake cleared his throat. "But I must tell you this . . . If by the end of the line we can't find anyone who will take both of you, we will have to separate you."

"No!" cried Kayla. "That we cannot let happen!"

Miss Ruth patted Kayla's arm. "We will pray for the right family. God is a miracle-worker."

Kayla nodded. In this mob of people it was hard to remember that God worked miracles. None of them believed it except herself, Timothy, Miss Ruth, and Mr. Stone. Mr. Drake called himself a Christian, but he said the day of miracles was past and that they'd better get used to it.

Several minutes later the train slowed to a stop in a small town in the middle of what seemed like a wilderness to the orphans used to New York City. Kayla liked the look of the tall trees and green hills with the small church standing in the valley. The sun shone brightly but wasn't hot. The depot was a small building almost on the train tracks. A crowd of people gathered to watch the train arrive. The children stared openly at the orphans. Several buggies and horses stood to one side of the depot.

Kayla's stomach knotted as she followed Timothy out of the boxcar. The orphans were as silent as the crowd that watched them line up.

"We will go to the same family, Timothy," whispered Kayla. "We won't have it any other way."

Timothy agreed. He rubbed his damp palms down his pants and tried to look bigger than he was. Would he never grow into a strapping big man like Papa had been? Timothy glanced at his new friend Del. He was thirteen, and he already wore the clothes and shoes of a man.

Mr. Drake stepped toward the crowd with a wide smile. "Ladies and gentlemen, I am Tom Drake of the Children's Aid Society. We have brought you the children we promised. We do want you to have a chance to speak to them and they to you. You may look at the children, then form a line, if you will, so that everyone has a chance to speak to the orphan who interests him."

Later a man stopped before Kayla, smiled, and said, "Hello. My name is Preston Jarvis, and this is my wife Peony. We talked over taking a big girl who could help us with our little ones."

"We have five," said Peony.

Kayla managed a smile. "My brother Timothy and I go together, sir."

The man scowled. "Irish? We don't want Irish. Drinking's in their blood."

Kayla's eyes snapped. "I am an O'Brian, and drinking is not in my blood! Not a one in my family has had the bottle touch their lips!"

Mr. Jarvis quickly moved on, but his wife smiled at Kayla and patted her hand.

Several people had heard Kayla, and she heard one of them say, "We don't want a girl who would sass. We'll pass her by."

Kayla lifted her chin higher. She had not meant to be

sassy, but she could not have the man blacken her good name.

Five children were taken, and one of them was Timothy's friend Del. Tears sparkling in his eyes, Timothy bade him farewell. Del sniffed and blinked hard, and Kayla knew he was ready to shed a tear as well.

Finally the people walked away, and the train was almost ready to roll. Kayla stood on firm ground as long as she could. She hated the constant movement of the train as much as she hated the clack and rumble of the wheels and the loud whistle.

Just then Kayla saw two boys peek around the corner of the depot. Were they orphans trying to run away? They saw her look at them, and they quickly ducked out of sight. She looked around for Timothy, but couldn't see him. A few of the children already stood inside the boxcar, but Timothy wasn't there. Maybe he'd gone to the spring that someone had mentioned to get fresh drinking water for all of them.

She ran to a tree where Miss Ruth was talking with Mr. Stone. "Miss Ruth!"

"Yes, Kayla?"

"Have you seen Timothy?"

She shook her head. "Have you, Wyatt?"

"Not since the crowd left."

Kayla's heart sank. "I'll run to the spring to see if he's there."

"Be sure to come back with the others even if you don't find Timothy," said Miss Ruth. "We'd hate to make the train wait for you."

Kayla lifted her skirts and ran across the grassy field to where she'd seen the others go for water. When she reached the spring she saw Apple, Clare, and Bobby and a few others she knew by name, but she didn't see Timothy.

Frantically she ran back toward the train. Had he run away? Or had someone who desperately wanted only a boy taken him? "Heavenly Father, please show me where my Timothy is!"

Suddenly a stone hit her leg just above her knee. She cried out in pain and almost fell. She grabbed her leg, hopping around as she tried to see who had hit her. Anger rushed through her and she yelled, "Whoever is doing this bad deed, step out and face me. Don't act the coward! Or are you afraid to face a girl?"

Two boys jumped into sight. They were the two boys she'd seen peek around the depot. She frowned. One boy had part of his left ear gone, and the other had a withered hand. They were both about six years old.

She shook her finger at them. "I know you. I know you both, you ragamuffins! You tried to rob Mr. Clements in the alley that day! You threw stones at his roan and made him buck until Mr. Clements lost his seat!"

"And we know you, Kayla O'Brian," cried the boy with the withered hand. "Me and Ear didn't eat that day because of you."

"You're gonna pay for what you did," said Ear. "Me and Louie have planned how we're gonna do it."

She shook her finger harder. "You boys have been throwing stones at me, scaring me with the snake, putting toads in my bag, doing all kinds of things to me all this time!" She stepped toward them, then saw the knife Ear had pulled out. Frantically she looked for help from Miss Ruth or one of the men, but they weren't in sight. "Put away the knife. Mr. Drake said you couldn't keep your weapons. The others left theirs behind." She took a steadying breath as she watched for even the slightest movement from Ear. "You are going toward a good life. Don't ruin it this way. Where you'll live you'll have plenty to eat, a place to sleep, and a family to care for you."

"We want what's due us from that mark in the alley," said Louie. "Give us what you took."

Kayla's eyes widened. "But I didn't take anything! Stealing is wrong! I chased you away so you wouldn't hurt or rob Mr. Clements."

"Was he a friend of yours?" asked Ear.

"I never saw him before that day."

"Then why'd you step in?" Louie stuck his withered hand behind his back as if he suddenly realized she could see it.

"I told you, stealing is wrong. The Bible says not to steal."

Puzzled, Ear shook his head. "I sure don't understand that. How can you stay alive on the streets if you don't steal?"

That she couldn't answer. "But now you never have to steal again," she said softly. "You'll have all you need. You saw those people today. In every place we stop there will be people who will want to adopt you."

Ear and Louie looked at each other as if they were reading each other's thoughts. Finally Ear slipped the knife back into his boot.

"We won't bother you no more," said Ear.

"You have our word on that," said Louie.

"All aboard!" yelled the conductor just then.

Relieved, Kayla watched the boys run across the grass and climb into the boxcar. She turned and looked around for Timothy. Just then she saw him running down the dusty street toward her.

She brushed an unsteady hand across her eyes and waited for him.

He pushed a peppermint stick into her hand. "That's for

you," he said. "I swept the floor of the store for two pieces of candy—one for you and one for me."

"Timothy, Timothy." She held her candy to her heart and scrambled into the boxcar with him.

Her Bible in her hands, Kayla stared at the spot where Apple had slept the past weeks. It was empty, and it made Kayla feel empty. A family had taken Apple at the last stop. During their time together Kayla had helped her quit swearing and had taught her about Jesus. "I will miss you, Apple," Kayla whispered. Her whisper was covered by the train's clatter and rumble and Mr. Drake's snoring. It was the middle of the day, and he had fallen asleep over his bookwork. Miss Ruth and Mr. Stone were talking quietly about the successful trip. The conductor had told them they could ride in the passenger car now that there were so few, but they chose to stay where they were. It was home — almost.

"Oh, Apple," whispered Kayla.

Apple had stood in line, her face scrubbed and her eyes bright with excitement. So far she'd not been taken because she was so small or in her excitement had let go with a string of swear words that had singed the ears of the families.

Kayla had watched a man and woman stop in front of Apple, and from the looks on their faces she knew they wanted Apple even if she was too small to do a day's work. Later they'd driven away with Apple on the woman's lap, her head on the woman's breast. Apple had found her home.

Two stops back Ear and Louie had been adopted by a big farmer with a loud voice. He'd taken them both even though they weren't family and he didn't have to. He'd wanted two boys because he already had three teenage daughters.

Bobby had been taken a while back when they first reached Iowa, but Clare couldn't go with him even though she'd cried loud and hard. She sat on her mat with her chin on her chest, her red hair in tangles. Once she'd tried to run away, but Mr. Drake had caught her and brought her back. She said she didn't want to live without Bobby.

At one stop just inside Nebraska a man had asked to take Clare, but when Miss Ruth found he was a widower she wouldn't allow it. The man had walked away in anger.

Reggy had gotten his heart's desire and had been taken by a family in town who owned the general store. He was proud that he could learn the trade. Kayla knew he would do well.

Kayla glanced over where Timothy sat with Mack, a boy from Scotland, swapping stories with him.

Timothy, Mack, Clare, and herself were the only ones left to find families. Several had wanted either Timothy or Kayla, but no one had wanted both. Now they were miles into Nebraska, the end of the line. If a family didn't take them soon, they'd have to be separated.

"That will not happen!" muttered Kayla.

She closed her Bible and pushed it back inside her bag. She touched Mama's diary. Could she read it today? Much of the pain over her loss was gone thanks to help from Miss Ruth and the time they spent reading and praying together.

Slowly Kayla lifted out the diary and stroked the cover. Her heart raced, and she almost pushed the diary back in place. Finally she opened it. Tears blurred her vision at the sight of Mama's neat script. She wiped away the tears and flipped further into the diary at random. Mama had written:

This has been a trying day for me. Patrick once again was cheated out of his share of the money. I am thankful I've taught Kayla and Timothy to forgive, for it is a hard lesson to learn when you're full-grown. Jesus said we must forgive or God can't forgive us—we block our fellowship with God. I must forgive. I must! With Jesus' help I do forgive. Oh, but it is hard to do! But I vowed that I wouldn't let anything keep me from serving and loving God with all my being.

Kayla looked up from the diary and across at Timothy. From the words she read, it was like Mama speaking to her. Mama indeed had taught them to forgive.

But they had not forgiven Hope Murphy.

It was impossible to forgive that woman. Kayla gritted her teeth. She could not forgive Hope Murphy! It was indeed impossible.

"Jesus says to forgive," Mama had said many times. "Unforgiveness is a sin, and that sin will ruin your life."

Kayla closed the diary and held it to her. She didn't want to ruin her life or allow Timothy to ruin his life just because they wanted to stay angry at Hope Murphy.

Kayla glanced across at Timothy, and he caught her eye. She motioned to him. He said something to Mack and crawled to her side. In whispers she told him what she'd read and the decision she'd reached. "We must forgive her, Timothy. We have no choice."

He set his jaw stubbornly.

"Mama said we must . . . Papa said we must . . . And, Timothy, Jesus said we must. So we must." Oh, but it hurt to say that! She felt she had every right to be angry and unforgiving . . . But right or not, Jesus said to forgive.

"An O'Brian obeys," whispered Kayla.

Timothy finally nodded. "You are right."

"I forgive Hope Murphy," said Kayla.

"I forgive her, too . . . with Jesus' help."

With their heads together they prayed softly, thanking Jesus for making their hearts pure and for helping them forgive.

At the next stop only two Nebraska families stood waiting for the orphan train. They took Mack and would've taken Timothy, but Miss Ruth explained why they couldn't. The other family wanted only a boy, so they drove away disappointed until the next orphan train came through.

The next day they rode with the boxcar door wide open. Warm Nebraska wind blew sand along as if it was having a race with the train. Kayla found no trees, only rolling hills and wide blue sky for as far as she could see. Riders on the range stopped to wave their wide-brimmed hats and shout a greeting.

"I like their horses," said Timothy, almost falling out onto the rails in his excitement.

"I do too." Kayla watched a pinto lope across the open prairie and wished she was riding it. Mr. Stone had told them many stories of brave, wonderful cowboys who rode the range.

Clare pouted in her corner, but she watched the riders too. Kayla knew that Clare was frightened that no one would take her.

Kayla twisted her braid around her finger. She and Timothy were also a little frightened. Not once had they thought that no one would adopt them, but with only two more stops they were beginning to wonder.

Late in the afternoon the train braked to a sudden stop, and Kayla lost her balance and flipped over, almost landing on Clare.

"What's wrong?" asked Mr. Drake, peering out the door.

Timothy leaped down before anyone could stop him. Kayla scrambled after him. Wind blew her dress tight against her body and flipped her braids. The engineer stuck his head out and yelled, "Cow on the track."

The fireman and the conductor pushed the cow off, and a few minutes later the train was on its way again. It was almost sundown when they stopped again.

Kayla smoothed her dress and flipped her braids back. She could tell Timothy and Clare were as nervous as she was. Clare had even taken the time to braid her hair to make herself more presentable.

In the dusk Kayla saw two families and a lone woman in a buggy waiting for the train. Kayla's tongue felt glued to the roof of her mouth, a problem she'd never experienced before. Her mind drifted as Mr. Drake gave the same speech he'd given at each stop. She knew it by heart. The two families stepped close, but the lone woman stayed in her buggy.

"These three all you got left?" asked one of the men as he pushed his hat to the back of his head.

"But three of the best," said Miss Ruth with a smile.

"I'll take that boy," said the man. "He's puny, but he's the only boy you got here."

"The boy goes with his sister," said Mr. Drake, pointing to Kayla.

"I don't have room for two," he said gruffly.

"We don't want two either," said the woman from the other family. "But we came for a boy."

The children stared at Kayla and Timothy as if they had two heads.

The woman stepped up to Clare. "Tell me about yourself, girl."

"I'm an orphan," said Clare coldly.

Miss Ruth stepped forward and filled the woman in on Clare's background and what she wanted in a family. The woman told about her family while her husband stood back without speaking a word. Her children, two small boys and a girl about eleven, stared at Clare.

"We'll take you if you want to come," said the woman to Clare.

Clare hesitated, then shrugged. "I'll come." She walked to the boxcar to get her things, while Miss Ruth filled out the necessary papers.

Kayla reached for Timothy's hand and laced her fingers through his. They were the only two left.

Just then the lone woman climbed from her buggy. Timothy whispered, "We'll be going with her."

"Oh!" said Kayla.

"I know 'tis true," he whispered.

Kayla trembled. Timothy had a way of knowing things, just like Mama had.

The woman walked toward them. She wore a faded calico dress, bonnet, and cowboy boots on her feet. She was quite tall and slender, with a determined look on her plain face. She stood in front of Kayla, but looked at the ground as she spoke. "I am Rachel Larsen. My man sent me to bring home a boy. We got two boys, fifteen and five, and two girls, eleven and six." She talked with a slight accent and as if words were hard to come by.

"They must go together," said Mr. Drake kindly but firmly.

Rachel Larsen looked at Mr. Drake and finally nodded.

"I will take them both. We live on a ranch and have plenty of room."

"You must see that they go to school," said Mr. Drake.

"They will get schooling."

"And to church."

"That too."

Kayla's heart thudded so hard, she was sure all of Nebraska could hear it. She felt Timothy tremble, but she couldn't turn her head to look at him. She felt frozen to the spot. This was the first time someone had to speak for her. Shyness had overcome others, but never her — until now.

In a hardy voice Mr. Drake told Mrs. Larsen about Kayla and Timothy. "They're fine youngsters. Well-mannered too."

"I will take them both," Rachel Larsen said again.

Mr. Drake turned to Kayla and Timothy. "Will you go with her?"

Kayla knew this was their last chance. The woman wanted them both. It was another miracle from God. Finally she nodded. She knew Timothy had too.

"Fine. It's settled." Mr. Drake smiled. "Get your things, and we'll fill out the papers."

Slowly as if in a dream Kayla followed Timothy to the boxcar. He handed her her case, and she took it. Rachel Larsen didn't look a bit like Mama, nor sound like her. But soon Rachel would be their mama.

"They live on a ranch," whispered Timothy. "That means they have horses."

"Horses?" whispered Kayla.

"God indeed answered for us. We will get to work with horses." From the time Mr. Stone had first talked about cowboys Timothy had wanted to be one.

Kayla nodded. Life would be different with a new mama

and papa, but they'd be living on a ranch with horses, and she knew about horses.

Miss Ruth hugged Kayla. "I wish you both the most wonderful life anyone could ever have!"

"I will miss you," whispered Kayla.

A few minutes later Kayla leaned against her case in the back of the buggy, with Timothy beside her. Rachel slapped the team with the reins, and the buggy rolled away — away from the train, away from Miss Ruth, Mr. Stone, and Mr. Drake — and out across the vast prairie that stretched on and on as far as Kayla could see.

Suddenly a bubble of excitement burst inside Kayla. She leaned toward Timothy and smiled. "We're going home," she said.